Lucifer and Mary Jane: All The Devil's Horses

A paranormal cozy romance novella

Laura Hesse

Running L Productions

Cover Design: Autumn Sky, SelfPubBookCovers.com
Publisher: Running L Productions Vancouver Island, British Columbia Canada
Publisher's Website: www.runninglproductions.com
Distributed Worldwide on Amazon

Contents

Pearly Gates

Hot breath fanned my face. It smelled faintly of apple and cinnamon oatmeal.

My chest felt like someone had shoved a red hot poker through it. I inhaled sharply and opened my eyes, too weak to sit up.

A soft grey and white muzzle nuzzled my cheek; wide flared nostrils sniffed my face. Dark warm eyes regarded me with concern.

"Hello, Mr. Jeepers," I mumbled as the elegant light grey dappled horse delicately chewed on a strand of my purple hair.

Another equine head nosed in, but this muzzle wasn't soft, it was as hard as bleached bone, which of course it was.

"Binky, that hurts," I eschewed Death's skeletal steed.

"What are you two doing here," I asked the two Hell horses looking down upon my prone form, "and where is Leyland?"

"Mary Jane," a soft masculine voice whispered in my ear. "Time to get up, sweetie."

"In all the realms, why would you bring her here," another male voice growled - this one not so caring.

I recognized the latter voice. It belonged to Saint Peter. Saint or no, he was as poisonous as a scorpion's sting. Dad threatened to cut off his arms once when Peter refused to let us through the Pearly Gates so my father could plead my case before God. I was little then, maybe three years-old, but I remember the cold hatred emanating from the guardian of the gate and his rich baritone voice as if it was yesterday. Not everyone in Heaven hated me, but many shared Saint Peter's opinion of Nephilims. Oh, did I mention that I was a Nephilim – a half-angel/half-human? Well, I am.

What was I doing at the gates and why was Saint Peter glowering at me, his expression smug, and his lips pressed together in a thin determined line?

Confusion clouded my mind. The last thing I remembered was galloping full tilt towards the water jump atop my bay gelding, Leyland, in the final lap of the National finals. Leyland and I had a chance of making the Olympic Eventing team. Scuttle butt at the horse show was that Leyland and I were a shoe-in. It was our last shot because Leyland was aging out and the Olympics were next summer. The large fine tuned Hanoverian cross had finally overcome his fear of water and we were sailing over the jump when everything went black.

Darn it, where was Leyland? And what were Mr. Jeepers, Binky, Death, the Grim Reaper, and Saint Peter doing in the middle of a three day equestrian eventing competition?

Pain coursed through my chest and abdomen as I sat up. The world canted sideways. Someone righted me before I toppled over.

"Sorry, Mary Jane," the Grim Reaper apologized, squatting down beside me. "I never thought I'd have to reap you."

"Don't worry about Leyland," Death crooned, not having to kneel beside me as he was a short man with an infectious smile, one that I dearly wanted to wipe off his face at the moment. Death looked a lot like Tyrion Lannister from Game of Thrones. He too had the ability to drink all who challenged him under the table, except for me and Zepar, the Grand Duke of the demon armies. I really liked Death, but Saint Peter's words had unnerved me.

"Your friend, Bernie, is looking after your horse. She's quite distraught. I'll pay her a little visit in her dreams tonight to see if I can cheer her up," Death smiled winningly.

He was so happy one would have thought he had just been chosen for the Olympic team and not me.

"Please don't," I wheezed, the pain in my chest making it hard to speak. The thought of Death paying a visit to one of my two best friends gave me the strength to sit up on my own. "I don't think Bernie would understand your humor. Besides, I can't die; I'm half angel, right?"

"I'm afraid you can if killed with the right instrument," Death replied, gently patting me on the shoulder. Mr. Jeepers, the Grim Reaper's steed, nosed Death, and then yanked hard on another strand of my hair. Death shrugged sympathetically and retrieved what was left of my shoulder length hair from the horse's mouth.

"Never thought I'd see the day I'd have to attend to you like this," the Grim Reaper moaned. "I mean, I thought Diana's arrows never left her chambers anymore, but there one is, embedded in your chest."

A long slender arrow made of dark polished wood with white swan feathered fletching pierced the center of my Kevlar safety vest. The Kevlar was impossibly strong which is why every event rider wore a vest to protect their ribcage in case of a serious fall. The sharp arrowhead protruded from my back having pierced my sternum. This was no easy feat considering the arrow had to travel through the Kevlar and the ample bosom squished beneath it.

No wonder it hurts to breathe.

"So I'm dead then," I stammered, fingering the arrow penetrating my heart. I felt stupid for even saying it, but at least the pain was receding.

"I'm afraid so," Death sighed.

"And we aren't quite sure what to do with you," the Grim Reaper agreed, his voice holding a note of sympathy. "Honestly, I thought the All Father would intervene."

"Yeah, don't hold your breath," I grimaced. "I'm not, but then I don't seem to be able to hold anything right now."

"I summoned Gabriel, but he has yet to make an appearance," Death ventured, clearly not amused.

"That's no surprise, I haven't seen daddy dearest in years."

"Well, you can't leave her here," Saint Peter spat. "I didn't open the gates for her as a babe and I won't now. She's an abomination!"

"I am not an abomination," I cried, suddenly realizing the seriousness of my situation. Angels and archangels didn't have souls, but they were children of Heaven so could come and go as they pleased. Humans had souls, and if they were judged good and true, Saint Peter would open the two intricately carved golden gates looming above us and let them pass. Being only half-human meant I only had half a soul, or so I've been told, and was not welcome inside those illustrious gates.

Heaven hated me, and God did too. At ten when my boobs started to sprout and my baby fat wasn't going away, the archangel Gabriel, my father, stopped coming to visit. My mother took it in stride, and told me if I couldn't be beautiful like her or my father, I needed to be smart. Unfortunately, I wasn't born an Einstein either. Bold and unpredictable was scribbled under my photo in my senior year high school yearbook – the editor was a friend and being nice. Three days before the horse show and my twenty-third birthday, I dyed my silver hair and wings amethyst. Ah, Captain Hindsight. Who knew the price of rebellion would be an eternity with wings and hair the color of a purple sea star?

My eyes burned. I would not cry in front of that supercilious sod, Saint Peter. I feigned a sneeze and rubbed the tears and snot from my nose at the same time. My poor blood covered safety shirt and blouse were now snotty too.

Self-pity overwhelmed me – loss for the horse I loved more than anything else in the world and for the two priceless friends left behind, for the Olympic Team I would never be a part of, and for the mother I never told how much I loved her near enough.

My worst fears had materialized: I was an unwanted child of an archangel, refused salvation, barred from Heaven, pitied by Death himself, and scorned by one of the most powerful saints in Heaven, so I did the only thing I could think of to do.

"UNCLE LUCIFER, I NEED YOUR HELP," I shrieked so loudly into the white and blue haze below me that Binky's bones blew apart, Mr. Jeepers staggered backwards several feet, and Death, the Grim Reaper, and Saint Peter tumbled backwards onto their buttocks.

Fallen Angels

"By all the demons' legions, Mary Jane," Lucifer snapped, his majestic onyx wings fanning out behind him as he strode purposefully towards the small group gathered in front of the golden gates. His black leather knee length duster custom built to accommodate his wings hung loosely at his sides. A dusty black Stetson partially covered his brown eyes and wavy blue-black hair. A lover of everything Old West, Lucifer's knee high brown leather cavalry boots were spit polished daily by Jesse James and his silver spurs jingled just like Brett Maverick's in the movies.

I always thought my uncle a dashing man rather than a fallen angel and ruler of the Underworld. The only time I was allowed to release my wings and fly was when I visited Hell. That was where I learned the difference between single malt and tequila, but don't tell my mother. Even at twenty-two, almost twenty-three, I was afraid of my mother's wrath.

"What in Heaven and Hell is all this caterwauling? A category six hurricane couldn't have done more damage. I didn't even have time to get Brimstone out of the field."

"I've been murdered," I sobbed. I hated crying in front of my uncle even more than in front of Saint Peter, but the tears wouldn't stop falling.

"It's true, sir, she has," the Grim Reaper squeaked.

"Aye, by one of Diana's arrows," Death nodded, not at all intimidated by the dark one's angry glare.

"I can see that for myself," Lucifer hissed, his eyes fixed upon the brilliant white fletched arrow in my chest.

"Who would want to kill me," I cried. "I've never done anything to anyone on Olympus. I just wanted to ride in the Olympics. I competed fairly and worked hard, so did Leyland."

Even to my ears, the whine in my voice was overwhelming.

"Stop crying, Mary Jane, you're stronger than that," Lucifer said, his stance and demeanor softening. "We'll figure it out. Where's your father? Gabriel should be here."

"I called him," Death said, coughing into his hand.

We all knew Gabriel wasn't coming. I was an ugly, beefy, big bosomed, tiny winged half-angel with a voice like a foghorn and two bricks short of a load. Like I said, I know who I am. I was an embarrassment to the mighty Gabriel, God's Herald.

"I see," Lucifer mumbled.

"She can't stay here," Saint Peter grumbled.

Lucifer shot him an icy look. Peter was wise enough not to comment further.

"Stand up, let's have a look at you," Lucifer commanded.

I wiped away my tears and stood up, straightening my shoulders as much as I could with a three foot arrow sticking out of my chest.

"Right, hold on to something," my uncle commanded as he lifted his foot and placed one boot beneath my boobs and wrapped his hands around the arrow's shaft intent on pulling the bolt straight through me.

My face must have shown my horror as Death raised one eyebrow and quipped rather stoically: "If I might suggest, my lord, perhaps we should break the arrow off at the back before you yank it out of your niece."

"Good point," Lucifer grinned.

The Grim Reaper stepped behind me and broke the shaft in two. Binky and Mr. Jeepers watched the proceedings with interest. I found some comfort in the two Hell horses standing beside me.

"Ready?" Uncle Lucifer asked.

I nodded, closing my eyes and preparing for the worst.

The devil yanked the shaft from my chest. It came out with an odd slurping squishy sound. Surprisingly it didn't hurt. Right away, I was able to stand straighter and thrust my boobs up and out once again. Marilyn Munroe would have been proud.

Lucifer examined the arrow in his hand, his eyes hooded. With a grunt, he handed the fletched part of the arrow to the Grim Reaper. "Take that back to Hell with you and drop it off in my office. No one is to touch it."

"Yes, sir," the Grim Reaper said, taking the shaft from the devil's hand. He nodded at me briefly before hopping onto Mr. Jeeper's back. In a flash, he and the Hell horse were gone. I was ever so glad my shout that blew Binky apart hadn't done the skeletal horse irreversible damage or hurt the magnificent grey that just disappeared in a puff of smoke.

"What do I do now," I sighed, looking helplessly at my uncle. "Where do I go if not through these gates?"

"The first thing you do is remove that silly vest and unfurl your wings," he smirked.

Saint Peter snickered as I took off the bloody vest and unfurled my small feathered wings. While they were a quarter size of the devil's and definitely not as glorious, they were still beautiful. I loved my short-stop wings. They were easier to hide and fit nicely under a t-shirt when I went swimming. Even my friends, Babs and Bernie, didn't know of their existence.

"Brilliant," Lucifer said cheerfully. "I don't recall ever meeting an angel with wings or hair that color. It makes you stand out."

"What now, uncle?" I frowned, still feeling a tad brittle despite his efforts to make light of the situation.

"You hold your head up high and fly back to Hell with me," Lucifer replied. "I'll find something for you to do. I'm not sure what, but we'll figure it out."

"I could work in the stable," I offered, my mood lifting. "I'm good with the horses and they like me. You know I'm not afraid of hard work. I don't want to be a freeloader or the girl that everyone says 'oh, look, there goes the brown-noser, the boss's niece'."

"I don't think anyone would dare say that to you, Mary Jane," Death laughed. "As I recall the last demon who offended you was found tied to a post in the main square, gagged and naked, with a sign around his neck reading 'spank me, baby'."

"He insulted Brimstone, not me," I said, twirling a strand of hair of gob-slobbered hair around one finger. "He was lucky it was only me who heard him."

Lucifer chuckled, his eyes gleaming.

"Yes, the stable is a good idea. I could use some reliable help and the generals won't feel put out by it. I can't insert you into one of their garrisons or add you to the torturers roster without a revolt and office work is not your strong suit."

"Office work, that would be hellacious," I agreed with a shudder, horrified at the thought of spending eternity filing paperwork? No, thank you.

"Ah, marvelous, it's settled then," Death said, clapping his hands together.

"You can't take her to Hell, Samael, she's neither demon nor human," Saint Peter seethed, using Lucifer's given name. "She has to go to Purgatory. That's the proper place for something like her."

Lucifer unsheathed his sword from beneath his duster and in one swift movement swung the blade towards Saint Peter's neck. The blade stopped a hair's width from its intended target. Flames rippled up and down both sides of the blade. Saint Peter's face blanched. He cowered, his back against the Pearly Gates. Somewhere behind the gates a series of ear-splitting trumpet blasts sounded.

"Don't ever tell me what to do again," Lucifer thundered, his eyes blackening, his handsome face hardening. "You can easily be replaced, Peter."

I took a step backwards. Like everyone else, I had heard tales of my uncle's anger, seen it fictionalized countless times in film, but had never seen it up close and personal until now.

"Nobody threatens my niece, not you, not even Heaven itself," my uncle growled, shielding his sword in one swift movement as two squadrons of armed angels flew in formation above us.

"That was worth the price of admission," Death chortled. He tapped Binky on the shoulder, and the horse bowed low enough for Death to leap onto his back. The deity saluted Saint Peter who now crouched against the gates, hands shielding his head and face, and quipped "Later, alligator."

I fought the urge to reply, 'In a while, crocodile'.

Lucifer spread his wings. I followed suit, albeit not so grandly.

The devil swan-dived off the platform we were standing upon, folding his wings tightly against his body. I wiped the silly grin off my face as the squadrons of angels dove dangerously close to us, releasing a cascade of silver and gold tipped arrows in our direction, as we plummeted down to earth.

Arrows whizzed by us.

One clipped my arm.

I screeched in pain as I tucked my wings against my back, clinging to my savior's side as the Prince of Hell's legions of demons rose out of Hell in a cacophony of fury and rage. I thanked the God who had forsaken me that the archangel in question was my Uncle Lucifer until I realized that I may have just started a war.

The Huntress

I had just left the stables after double-checking on Beetle, the young demon of indeterminate heritage with no wings and a face that only a mother could love if his mother hadn't abandoned him at birth. Beetle was a good lad, but his smile would scare Frankenstein. Beetle smiled a lot so it was something I was going to have to get used to. Still, I liked him. He was reliable, unlike Chappie, the other stable hand.

I was tired, but ready for a pint.

Dying took a lot out of me.

Chappie left a long list of abandoned chores behind him, preferring the pub to work. He had sneaked out without warning. Chappie was an arrogant sod, an Aussie bandit who fancied himself a member of the illustrious Kelly gang, which he was not. I wasn't violent, but one day I was going to sic Brimstone, Lucifer's prize stallion, on him. That would wipe the sneer off the groom's face.

It was late by the time Beetle and I finished all of Chappie's chores and our own.

King Zagan's legions of drunken bloodthirsty demons overwhelmed the taverns and streets of Hell Town. Winged demons staggered about spewing forth imaginary exploits. Even from outside the Hellfire Stables, I could hear their singing and excessive recounting of their bravery in the face of the squadrons of heavenly angels that chased my uncle and I right down to the River Styx. Both Death and King Zagan had invited me to join them for a pint at the Satyr Pub to celebrate the short if not bloody skirmish.

I had balked at first, but knew that Chappie would be there trying to weasel his way into King Zagan's good graces. I intended to thwart his efforts. I know, I should play nice, but his nasty comment after Uncle Lucifer left me alone in the loft with him still angered me.

"Poor little Nephilim can't get into Heaven, boohoo," the unruly ragged stable boy hissed, his Aussie accent thick with condemnation. "Ya think you're something because the devil's yer uncle. Well you're not, are ya? You're worse than me. Least I got a soul. You're just a bloody bogan."

Later on, I asked Beetle what a bogan was. He said he didn't know, but Chappie called him that all the time too.

I assumed being called a bogan was an insult: so much for fitting in at the Hellfire Stables.

Duke Zepar and his mounted legions were patrolling Hell's borders lest the archangel Michael decided to use my dilemma as a means of starting a full out war between Heaven and Hell. The skirmish between demon and angel lasted only an hour. Losses were minimal on both sides, all things considered, and I was glad of that. Not all the angels in Heaven hated me; at least, I don't think they did. It would be horrible to lose someone I didn't know who might actually be on my side. After all, I wasn't the only Nephilim in existence.

I had given each horse one last pat, giving an extra ladleful of grain to Brimstone and Mr. Jeepers. Half the stable was empty since many of the dukes were out patrolling on their horses with Duke Zepar.

Before I hit the pub, I wanted to assure Uncle Lucifer that my transition to Head Groom in his stable had gone without a hitch, which it hadn't, but I wasn't one to complain to the Prince of Darkness. I also wanted to thank him one more time. Seriously, without him, I'd be aimlessly wandering around Purgatory, now and forever more.

I strode up the cobblestone path to his mansion. The four guards at the gate high-fived me, grinning like jack o'lanterns as they opened the solid iron doors for me. I had to use my wings to stay on my feet as one of them slapped me on the back so hard I almost hit the stone walkway. I wasn't sure I liked this celebrity status.

Lights were on in the den on the ground floor of the sprawling lava rock mansion. The roaring fire captivated my attention as I passed by the open window on the way to the side entrance, the dancing flames mesmerizing in their intensity. Fire was always more intense in Hell.

I stopped and looked inside. Lucifer sat in front of the rock walled fireplace, his boots resting on a padded stool, his silver spurs digging into the fabric. He stared into the flames, a glass of whiskey in one hand, his brow furrowed in thought. I was about to lean through the window and shout 'boo', but then I heard him whisper: "What shall I do with you, Mary Jane? You are a conundrum."

He snorted back a laugh as if finding the whole situation rather amusing: God's Herald's daughter living in Hell, mucking out stalls, sleeping on a cot in the barn loft, and possibly celebrating her downfall with Death at the Satyr Pub.

I knew what my uncle was thinking. I wasn't daft. I moved quickly into the shadows as a knock on the door startled Lucifer out of his reverie.

"Sir, the huntress is here," his demon servant announced with disdain.

"Interesting," he said.

His eyes blackened like they did when he was angry, and his gaze became reflective, a crooked smile forming on his lips. The smile unsettled me the most.

"Let her in."

Diana swept into the room with an angry flourish. She wore a richly embroidered shimmering knee length white and gold smock that was split to the waist at the sides, leather breeches, and tall boots. Her face was purple with rage. Her sling of arrows was cross-tied over her shoulders and she held her long wooden bow like a lance in one hand.

"Is it true?" the goddess seethed. "Was one of my arrows used to kill a half-breed?"

Lucifer waved her towards the table across the room where the two halves of the arrow that killed me sat upon a red velvet pillow as if they were the crown jewels.

Diana strode towards the scarred oak table, picked up the section of arrow with the fletching, and compared it to one of the others from her quiver. Her tanned face whitened.

Lucifer admired the sway of her hips and the sun-kissed luster of her long golden hair as she stood there, silent. From my shadowed hiding place outside the mansion, I could see the huntress was making my uncle's blood boil, not with anger, but lust.

Were they involved? Huh! If they were, did that mean my uncle may have had something to do with my murder?

I quickly let the last thought go. It was too painful to even consider.

"Come, sit," he said to Diana, motioning to her once again. The winged back chair across from him sat empty.

"This isn't a social visit, Lucifer," she growled.

"I know," he sighed, his eyes returning to brown.

Diana grunted and laid the broken arrow back down upon the table before striding forward with panther like grace.

"Who had access to your quiver on Olympus," the devil inquired before taking a sip of whiskey.

"Everyone," she sighed wearily, slumping into the chair. "It's not like there is much happening anymore. We've been so long forgotten that Olympus is fading. Many of the gods have already passed on, not wanting to linger in a world that fancies them as nothing more than characters in a video game."

"If it's any consolation, it has started here as well," Lucifer confessed.

What? Hell fading?

That was news to me.

"Drink?"

"No, Luci, I'm not staying," she whispered, her gaze fastened upon my uncle's.

"Too bad," he murmured, turning on the charm.

"Why would someone want to murder your niece with one of my arrows?" Diana asked, her cheeks reddening. "There are better ways to start a war than that, surely?"

"Are there," the devil countered, for indeed that was the thought that troubled me as well.

"Don't shoot me down," the goddess grumbled. "You always do that."

"I'm not shooting you down, I'm agreeing with you," Lucifer smirked. "I've been trying to figure it out all night. Could it be as simple as someone wants to start a war between Heaven and Hell?"

"If so, it triggered a one hour war," Diana smiled maliciously. "I'm disappointed in you; you usually last longer than that."

I held my breath. My uncle had a short fuse. I was about to launch into my 'boo', wanting for some reason to save the goddess from his wrath, but he surprised me with a hearty laugh instead.

"I confess, it felt good to unleash Zagan and his thirty-three legions. It has been eons since they'd had a good battle. The legions are growing complacent. There are rumblings of a major revolt. They thought I didn't know. Fools! I have spies everywhere."

Oh, oh, I winced.

Unrest?

Revolts?

Would I be a target for an angry mob because I was the big guy's niece?

I hadn't thought of that. Of course, I never thought I'd be murdered either.

"Regardless, I now have a good reason to visit Olympus and a dependable new stable hand. My stallion is thrilled. He dotes on the girl as do all the rest of the Hell horses. She has a way with them. I think you'll like her."

"Is it true she is ugly and has teeny tiny eggplant colored wings?" Diana giggled.

Okay, now I wished Uncle Lucifer had lost it on her.

"Alas, it is," he exhaled slowly, a twinkle in his eye. "Why don't you stay the night and I'll introduce you two at breakfast?"

"Ooooh, you are an evil one," Diana said, uncoiling herself from the chair.

That was enough for me. The Satyr Pub, here I come.

Celebrity Blues

I entered the pub to a chorus of "Mary Jane" and "I want'a buy ya a drink", once again dodging claw after claw as every soldier in the place wanted to congratulate me for starting what Diana called the *One Hour War*. My back, shoulders, and wings were mottled with bruises and scratches. I felt like the drum in a high school marching band.

To be honest, it was awkward being the subject of so much adoration by crowds of red and black faced toothy demons, some with black leathery wings, others with long braids of angel and human hair swinging from their belts, all with foul breath and fiery eyes. Their eyes were only red when they were consumed with blood lust. I squared my shoulders and tried to look brave.

I'd always loved Hell Town with its witches shops, apothecaries, blacksmith forges, armories, casinos, funky breweries, and hedonistic establishments. It was loud, fun, and full of wonders, some amazing and others, such as those selling implements to torture souls, that were utterly terrifying. Tonight, lanterns cast a ghoulish glow on the hundreds, if not thousands, of revelers.

I was four years-old the first time I visited Hell Town. My mother had dug up an incantation spell on the internet to summon the devil and it actually worked; although, Lucifer told me years later it was only because he had heard about my mother and her half-breed child that he decided to answer it. Even then it was mostly out of curiosity. When he arrived at our house, he discovered a tiny winged child flying around the room, bouncing off walls, and throwing an archangel sized tantrum. The tantrum was the result of being turned away from Heaven the first time.

The memory still made me sad.

Lucifer was so taken with my mother – she had that effect on men – he agreed to take me off her hands for a few days. I fell instantly in love with my dashing uncle and his glorious stable of horses. My uncle rode Brimstone through the cobbled streets of Hell Town with me sitting in the saddle in front of him.

I was startled out of my reverie by Geryon, the tallest and most powerful of centaurs and guardian of Hell's gates.

"Well done, Mary Jane," he rumbled, yet again slapping me on the back. I tumbled forwards into a group of demons. "I always knew you belonged here."

What was it with everyone wanting to manhandle me? And why did he think I belonged in Hell?

"Uh, thanks, Geryon," I stammered, intimidated by the enormity of the massive torso and powerful hind quarters.

Geryon grinned and sauntered off towards one of the casinos. I thought better than to ask if he was out gambling who was guarding the gates to Hell.

"Ho, ho, ho," a demon joked to his friends. "It's the little lady who got us blooded at last."

The small group of young demons looked at me with worship in their eyes. I blushed and quickly ducked into the Satyr Pub, slamming headlong into the king's guardsmen who were blocking the door.

"Let the lady through," Death yelled when the self-elected bouncers barred my way.

The soldiers and pub patrons ignored him. If I wasn't dead already, surely the crush of demons, guardsmen, soldiers and Hell's denizens outside the pub fighting to get in would have crushed me. I held my breath at the stink of demon flesh, alcohol, tobacco and sweat, stuck as I was between the battalions of party goers.

What was I thinking in coming here?

I caught a glimpse of Chappie at the bar. He smirked and held up his drink in salute. It wasn't a kind gesture.

"LET HER THROUGH," Death bellowed, climbing on top of the bar to make himself heard.

"Enough," King Zagan commanded. "Stand aside for Mary Jane,

newest member of Hell's fighting forces!"

The room went silent. The masses parted. I tucked in my lavender wings and smiled, nodding at several demons I recognized as I passed by. I smirked to myself – my wings were lavender in color, not eggplant like Diana had insinuated.

Wait! Did Zagan just call me the 'newest member of Hell's fighting forces'?

I was in serious trouble.

King Zagan towered over me. He was at least eight feet tall, his wings when fully extended being close to fifteen feet. At the moment, those giant black thin leathery wonders of Hell swept the floor clean at his feet, the barbed tops towering another foot over his wide boney head. He was a lying thieving scoundrel and the most powerful demon in Hell. I reminded myself of that as I approached him with the proper deference. Had I not, hero or no, the generals gathered around him would have torn me apart.

Chappie grinned maliciously at me from the end of the bar. I would have flipped Chappie the bird, but three of the king's generals flanked him and they might think I was aiming the rude gesture at them.

"Hail to Mary Jane," the king announced, lifting his glass. "Thanks to her we spilled blood today... angel blood!"

A rousing cheer went up.

The king winked and then turned his back on me in dismissal. That was just like Zagan, but better to be ignored by him than the focus of his attention.

"Pint or shot?" Death asked.

"Anything so long as it dulls the pain," I whispered hoarsely.

"Of what," Death chuckled. "Don't you like being a celebrated bringer of war to the masses?"

"No, I don't," I said, punching my friend lightly in the arm. "Every muscle in my body hurts. Between being murdered, thrown out of Heaven, falling from grace, and mucking out twenty-two stalls, and then getting manhandled by every demon in Hell Town, there isn't one part of my body that isn't sore."

"Poor baby," Death teased from his seat on the bar. He swung his legs like a toddler, putting his boot into the chest of a drunken guardsman who stumbled towards me. The guardsman eyed me like a tasty treat.

I swatted Death playfully in the arm, warming at the brotherly affection he'd always shown me. Not that he was my brother, Death being at least two thousand years-old, but he felt like it all the same. He once told me he wasn't the first Death, but didn't elaborate more than that.

"Whiskey for my girl," he called to the bartender.

"Make it a double," I said, rubbing my shoulder where one amorous demon had taken a nip out of me.

Maybe I really should have gone to Purgatory. All the attention and intrigue were giving me a headache.

The bartender slid a double whiskey down the bar. I caught it and glanced up, my gaze meeting that of a street urchin in the faded mirror above the bar. Sunken eyes, hair looking as if she'd stuck a finger in a light socket, off-kilter wings, and dried bloodstains on a once crisp white blouse. I'd have to go shopping for new clothes in the morning. That urchin was me.

"All's well that ends well, sweetie," Death laughed, lifting his glass of whiskey in a toast.

I downed my shot and leaned in to whisper in my friend's ear, "Would you walk me home after the next one? With Death at my side, no one will bother me. I'm tired of getting mauled. It has been an awfully long day."

"Party pooper," my friend giggled drunkenly, wrapping an arm around my wounded shoulder. "You have nothing to fear here, my sweet Mary Jane, Hell loves you. The prince loves you. I love you. Why even the king loves you tonight."

"Did you just say you loved me," I gaped. "I think you've had enough to drink."

"Probably true," he grinned. "Come on then, you've made your entrance. Let's go back to your place and drink some more... where it's safe. I'll sleep in the stable with Binky. The one good thing about owning a bone horse is there's no manure to wake up coated in."

I rolled my eyes and helped Death off the bar not entirely sure he would be able to stand let alone walk back to the stables.

Once again, I found myself being jostled about as Death and I struggled to get out of the Satyr Pub.

There are no clocks in Hell; there doesn't need to be. When in Hell, one is on Hell's time, which is endless. I had no idea how long it had been since I was killed upside and landed in the Underworld. Life in the fast lane I guess. Regardless, the streets of Hell Town were littered with staggering demons and lost souls. One poor sot had crawled into a fountain and passed out in the arms of a stone centaur.

I missed my mom, but Lucifer assured me I would be able to see her when she came down to teach her spin class. The demons loved her. I think one of the king's generals had a thing for her since he was always in her class, his guardsmen forced to endure my mother's particular brand of torture for hours.

I missed Leyland terribly, but it would be unfair to ask my uncle if I could retrieve my horse and unfair to Leyland as well.

I missed my friends. Eventually, they would move on with their lives and forget about me.

"That bench looks comfy," Death croaked, breaking away from me. He lurched forward as if caught in an invisible wind. I grabbed him by the arm and righted him before he landed face first into the centaur fountain.

"You know I think I can make it from here," I chuckled, leading him towards a vacant bench. Most benches were already occupied by sleeping revelers.

Death grunted as he fell in a heap onto the bench. I lifted his legs and tucked his coat around him.

"Comfy?" I asked.

"Delightfully so," he murmured and then was fast asleep.

I knew he would be alright. One doesn't mess with Death.

I skirted the main drag which was still quite busy, keeping to the back streets until I reached my uncle's home. The two storey mansion had a classic Greek fountain in the front with a wide terrazzo and a statue of Lucifer on his stallion rearing above the gates. Unseen from the front were beautiful rose gardens and a giant cedar hedged maze in the back. One could ride two horses abreast in the maze. The River Styx meandered past the farthest side of the property. It was a beautiful river stocked with trout and wild salmon. Not everything in the Underworld was bad.

I wasn't sure if Lucifer would bring the goddess Diana to the stables to meet me in the morning and decided on the spot to leave the whiskey bottle beneath my bed unopened. Embarrassing my uncle in front of his flame wasn't something I wanted to do even if the tiny devil on my own shoulder urged me to see how far I could push it in this new home of mine.

The guards waved at me as I crossed the front entry and I waved back. My riding boots' heels clicked on the cobblestones. I pushed my frizzy hair out of my face, the humidity in Hell making it stand to attention. While my hair stood on end, my wings drooped. Tiredness and the burn of whiskey in my gullet made me stumble.

I stopped to look down at the grand dame of all stables. The Hellfire Stables consisted of two buildings, the main building housing Lucifer's four horses including Brimstone, Charlemagne, Styx and Diablo, plus Binky, Mr. Jeepers, Bucephalus (yes, that Bucephalus, once owned by Alexander the Great but won in a poker game by Duke Zepar), Wild Fire, Duke Berith's red stallion, plus a palomino gelding owned by Plague, and a great black steed owned by the One-With-No-Name, also known as the anti-Christ, who I had yet to meet and hoped never to. The other stable housed various dukes and generals horses, but their soldiers took care of them. The cavalry's stables were elsewhere.

The stable was a magnificent two storey affair of stone and iron, built in the gothic style. The roof was red slate, the stone a light gold. Two giant sliding doors made of oak covered the front entry way. There was a winding iron staircase leading into the hay loft where the grooms bunkhouse room and stable manager's suite was located. I was fortunate enough to be given the suite. It wasn't luxurious by any means, but it had a single bed, wash sink and English style loo with a pull cord toilet.

As I stood looking down at the darkened stable beneath the

crimson skies of Hell I wondered if Lucifer and Diana were correct in their assumption that I may have been murdered to start a war. Or, was it that someone on earth wanted me out of the equation? Maybe somebody discovered I was a Nephilim and didn't want a half-angel on the Olympic Eventing Team? Maybe one of the Gods on Olympus didn't like that idea? Jealousy was an ugly thing. I could think of a few riders who begrudged Leyland and me our hard work and success too. The list of possible killers seemed endless.

How in Heaven and Hell did that happen?

As I descended the few steps to the stable yard I felt the hair go up on the back of my neck. Something was wrong. It took a minute for me to figure it out. There was no light burning outside the tack room and the upstairs light in the loft was also off as well.

Where was Beetle?

I knew Chappie was still at the pub rubbing shoulders with the high and mighty.

Unease made pimples rise on my skin. Geryon was gambling; perhaps the gates to the underworld really were left unguarded.

I slipped quietly through the stable's double doors and stood listening. Sounds were muffled. A few horses munched on hay, but for the most part, it was quiet.

I flipped on the light on the wall by the double doors. The stable's bright sodium lights hummed into life. Four stall doors hung open.

My blood, which was already running cold, turned to ice. The brass name plaques on the open stall doors read: Styx, Diablo, Mr. Jeepers and Binky.

"Hell's bells," I swore, racing to the empty stalls.

There was no trace of the horses and no signs of distress. Everything was neat and tidy except for the hoof prints in the sawdust and piles of uneaten hay.

Death was passed out on a park bench. Lucifer was with Diana doing only the devil knew what. The Grim Reaper may have taken Mr. Jeepers but he would have left a note on the chalk board by the tack room if he had. He was meticulous about that. So, who took the horses?

Brimstone whinnied shrilly and banged a leg against his stall door. I ran to the stallion's side. Beetle lay unconscious in the corner of Brimstone's stall, a giant bruise forming on his temple, the lizard like skin on his head split open to reveal the bone protrusions of his newly forming stubby horns. Beetle wasn't old enough to have a full set of horns yet.

"Beetle," I cried, throwing open the door and stepping inside.

Beetle moaned.

The great black stallion nipped my arm, his muscular neck arched, his luxurious mane brushing my shoulder.

"Did you do that or did someone else do it?" I asked the horse.

Brimstone snorted, sending gobs of mucous into my face.

"Ugh," I stammered, pushing the stallion's nose away from me.

"Mary Jane," Beetle mumbled.

"It's okay, I'm here," I replied rather stupidly, kneeling beside him. It wasn't okay, was it? "What happened, Beetle?"

"I tried to stop them," he cried, "but they were too big."

"Who were?"

"The men," he sobbed. "One of them was dressed like an angel. He had a sword and everything but he was no angel. He was a man. They tried to take Brimstone but he protected me instead."

The stallion snorted.

"How long ago was this," I asked him, trying to comfort the young demon by gently stroking his back.

"I dunno," Beetle whined.

"Hang on, Beetle, I'm going to call my uncle," I consoled him. "Brimstone, be a good boy and watch over Beetle."

"The boss is going to kill me," Beetle wailed.

"No, he won't, I suspect he'll give you a medal for trying to stop the bandits all on your own."

The stallion nodded in agreement. It didn't surprise me. Brimstone loved Beetle as much as he loved Lucifer.

I quickly exited Brimstone's stall, locked it behind me, and ran to the tack room. There was a buzzer on the wall that was only meant to be used in case of emergencies. If this wasn't an emergency, what was?

I pressed the buzzer, but nobody picked up at the other end of the line. An alarm was supposed to ring in the guard tower and in Lucifer's office at the same time.

I bit my lip and pressed the buzzer again.

This was serious.

Should I run up to the guard tower?

That might give the horse thieves even more time to escape.

Should I saddle Brimstone and see if I could find them?

No, Lucifer wouldn't like that. Besides, it would be one against four and Beetle was stronger than me. I'd be pummeled.

I pressed the buzzer one last time. Still, nobody answered my call. I looked at the fire alarm beside the buzzer. It took only a couple of seconds for me to decide what to do.

I pulled the fire alarm.

Sirens blared, and then all Hell broke loose!

911

It looked like a tide of Christmas Island red crabs, the numbers of demons scrambling down the small hill towards the stable so huge that within a couple of minutes of sounding the fire alarm there wasn't an inch of ground left to stand on.

Two fire trucks flew down the cobblestone path, lights and sirens blazing. Scores of demons were run over.

It seemed as if everyone in Hell had answered my call.

A shirtless Lucifer wearing only jeans and cowboy boots raced down the hill, the gorgeous goddess Diana on his heels. She had managed to throw a peach colored sarong over her doe skin leggings and boots. Her sling of arrows and bow rested against her back.

"Where's the fire?" Lucifer demanded. His eyes and hair were wild and tussled. "I don't see any flames?"

"I'm sssssorry," I stuttered, blushing from head to toe. "There is no fire."

"Is this some kind of a joke," Lucifer bellowed in my face, his eyes blazing as red as the fire engines.

"No," I croaked. "It's worse than a fire."

"By all the Gods, what is worse than a fire," Diana quipped, eying me with dislike.

I instantly knew the huntress and I were never going to get along.

"Styx, Diablo, Mr. Jeepers and Binky are missing," I seethed staring Diana down. She was only a visitor here, whether she came from Lucifer's bed or not. "Four men, human men, one dressed up as an angel, took them and beat up Beetle when he tried to stop them. He's barely conscious. Brimstone's watching over him."

"Did I hear you say someone beat up Beetle and my trusty steed has been stolen," Death asked, stumbling through the crowd.

"Yes, you did," I said more confidently. "We need to catch those horse thieves before they get to the gates."

Lucifer harrumphed and spun on his heel. His eyes still glowed with hellfire.

Geryon cantered past the fire trucks and bulldozed his way through the crowd of angry demons passing along news of the horse theft. I've never seen a centaur look alarmed, but fear, contrition, and anger played across Geryon's face in a flash of understanding. He had been derelict in his duties. Geryon had left the gates unmanned thinking the armies were still patrolling the perimeter, but obviously they were not.

"You heard my niece, find my horses and bring the horse thieves back to me alive!" Lucifer spat, spittle flying. The slick scratch of swords on leather rent the air as demon after demon drew their weapons, their eyes flaring up once again with blood lust. This time it wasn't angel blood they sought, it was human. I shuddered; glad it was not me they were after.

"And you," Lucifer sneered, waving a hand in the giant centaur's direction. "I will deal with you later. Get back to your post and close those gates!"

"Yes, my Lord," Geryon bowed. He reared and galloped ahead of the army of demons chasing down the scent of the horse thieves.

The thunderous sound of a thousand demons charging across the plains filled me with awe. The ground trembled beneath my feet.

Hell reacted to Lucifer's mood. Volcanoes exploded, spewing ash into the air, lava fireballs shooting upwards into the starless night. The tortured souls in the far off camps screamed in pain. I cringed at the horror of it all.

"Care to hunt," Lucifer asked Diana.

"Do you really need to ask," she laughed.

"Bridle up Brimstone and Charlemagne," he ordered me. "No saddles. Get Doc Holiday to look after Beetle."

I raced to the tack room, snatched Brimstone's and Charlemagne's bridles off the rack and bolted back to Brimstone's stall. By the time I got there, Lucifer and Diana were waiting, Diana tapping her foot impatiently.

Lucifer snatched Brimstone's bridle out of my hand and threw open the stall door.

"Let's find your brothers," Lucifer told the stallion without so much as a glance towards the injured young demon huddled in the corner.

By the time Lucifer had the bridle on Brimstone, I was slipping a bridle over Charlemagne's head.

Diana stood in the aisle eyes full of contempt.

Charlemagne was a draft warhorse, a massive dappled grey with a flowing black mane and tail, intelligent eyes, elegant of carriage, and broad of haunch and shoulder. His coat was darker than Mr. Jeepers. He had carried Lucifer throughout the Middle Ages in campaign after campaign.

"Good boy," I told the warhorse.

Charlemagne danced on the spot, eager to be off. It had been at least three hundred years since he had been called into service. Excitement rippled through his muscles as Diana led him out of the stable behind Lucifer and Brimstone.

Diana leapt aboard him as if he was no taller than a pony. She jerked on the reins causing Charlemagne to rear and strike out. Her anger was with me not the horse. Rage set my wings to trembling which caused her to smirk. If she thought I feared her, she was mistaken. I spent half my life in Hell. There was good along with evil in its streets. I had learned early on to embrace the good and set aside the horrors that Man, rather than God had created, but that was a different story.

Lucifer vaulted effortlessly onto Brimstone's back. "I'll deal with you when I get back too," Lucifer scolded me.

He loosened the reins and Brimstone shot forward into a gallop, sparks flying off the cobblestones.

Diana whirled Charlemagne in a circle. Charlemagne's eyes were wide, his ears pinned back in anger. She shot me a defiant look before letting the warhorse loose. I hoped Charlemagne would dump the goddess on her illustrious butt before the ride was over.

"You're deep in it, aren't ya," Chappie snorted as he sauntered towards me. "It was your watch."

"Actually, it was yours," I growled.

He shrugged with indifference.

"Go get Doc Holiday," I commanded. "Beetle's hurt."

"What do I care? Yer not my boss," he snorted, heading for the stairs to the loft.

"Yes, I am," I rounded on him.

"You'd better listen, boy," Death hissed, walking out of the shadows. "If you don't, you'll answer to more than just me."

Chappie snarled at Death, bearing his teeth, more like a demon than a lost soul.

"One day, nobody will be here ta protect ya," Chappie threatened, before stalking off towards Doc Holiday's cottage. The cottage was located on the north end of the stable grounds beside the outer gate to Main Street, Doc Holiday being both a doctor for Hell's royalty and veterinarian for their horses.

"I hope Lucifer fires him," I sighed. "Beetle and I did all his chores plus our own."

"Chappie's not worth your time, but you do need to be careful, he's got it in for you," Death consoled me. "There's a reason he's in Hell. As far as I know, you can't be killed twice, but you can be hurt and there are those here powerful enough to obliterate your half-soul."

"I'll keep that in mind," I agreed, gulping down the lump of unease that settled in my chest like a bad case of heartburn.

There was a loud moan from Brimstone's stall.

"Oh, gosh, poor Beetle," I cried, running back into the barn, Death on my heels.

I knelt in the sawdust and cradled Beetle's head against my chest. Tears poured from the young demon's eyes as blood continued to weep out of his head wound. My heart broke for him. He was so brave.

"Now I am jealous," Death sighed longingly.

I rolled my eyes at my friend. When Death was born, the average man stood about five feet tall and Death was just under that. I was big boned, ample bosomed and stood six foot three inches in riding boots so I towered over him, that is when I was kneeling cradling a demon against my bosom.

"You should be worrying about Binky and the other horses not having lascivious thoughts about me," I chastised him.

"Binky will find his way home," he chuckled. "I think he's enjoying the adventure. I wouldn't be surprised if Mr. Jeepers and the other two are too. Lucifer has been ignoring Styx and Diablo in favor of Brimstone for far too long, Charlemagne too for that matter."

"You think the horses went off of their own accord?" I gasped.

"Hmmm, you know we need to find you a boyfriend," Death joked, changing the subject.

If he were standing a little closer, I would have swatted him.

Find a boyfriend in Hell?

Seriously, that was a depressing thought. Who was I going to date... a demon... a wraith... a lost soul... some arrogant deity or fallen angel?

And then it hit me: *I was going to be single for eternity!* Now that was a depressing thought.

For a moment, tiredness sloughed off me and I forgot all about the stolen horses and the injured demon in my lap and thought only of my pathetic future, until Doc Holiday strolled in, a lit cigarillo hanging out of the side of his mouth. Okay, now that was a man I could date!

Doc Holiday

I hadn't seen Doc Holiday since my sixteenth birthday when Uncle Lucifer threw a party for me at the Satyr Pub. Lucifer had said something about it being legal in England so he plied me with all kinds of booze. I found out a few years later that only wine and beer was legal at sixteen in England. My mother had come down for the occasion too.

For awhile I thought Uncle Lucifer and my mother were having a fling. I asked her once about it, but she gave me a look that clearly said it was none of my business.

The party had the desired effect; I was so sick for three days afterwards I didn't touch a drop of liquor for the next five years. Sometimes I think Lucifer and my mother planned it that way.

Anyway, I digress.

Before me stood one of the most illustrious men in human history – Doc Holiday. Doc Holiday was a handsome man. His black hair and sweeping moustache were trimmed neatly. He was of medium height, slim, athletic, and had piercing brown eyes that missed nothing. A wine tipped stubby cigarillo hung out of his mouth. A gold pocket watch was tucked inside the pocket of a dark paisley vest, his white shirt was starched straight, his grey jacket was short armed and narrow waisted. Behind him skulked the want-to-be Billy the Kid Aussie stable hand.

"Doc," Death nodded.

"Death," he drawled in a southwestern accent. "What have we got here, Mary Jane?"

"Beetle got beat over the head by a bunch of horse thieves," I stammered, my heart racing at the carnal thoughts that popped into my head, Doc Holiday being the center of them.

Death chuckled under his breath.

I shot him a warning glance.

"I heard," Doc scowled, dropping his old fashioned leather doctor's bag on the ground beside me as he knelt to examine Beetle.

"My head hurts," Beetle whimpered. "Why'd they hit me so hard, Doc?"

"Because you're a brave young demon," Doc smiled.

"See, Doc agrees with me," I grinned encouragingly.

Beetle beamed until the Doc probed the open wound. Beetle cringed, but to his credit, he didn't yelp. Thankfully the blood had started to clot and the bleeding had slowed. Still, it was an ugly thing to see and I felt for the young lad.

"This is going to hurt, Beetle, but it has to be done," Doc said gently as he took a mickey of whiskey out of his bag and soaked the end of a clean cloth with it. "Hold him tight, Mary Jane."

I wrapped my arms around Beetle's quivering body, his snake-like demon skin hot to the touch while it should have been cold. Beetle shrieked in pain when Doc Holiday touched the cloth to the head wound, his bravado evaporating.

"There, there, all done my boy," Doc said as he stuffed the stained cloth inside a pouch and retrieved a roll of white bandages. He skillfully wrapped the demon's head wound, and then gave Beetle a dose of laudanum to dull the pain.

"That is quite the crack on the noggin," he remarked. "I want you to stay in bed for two days and then only light chores for a few days after that. I know you demons are a tough lot, but you aren't invincible."

The last part was directed at me. Even Doc knew that Chappie was hopeless.

Chappie was about to complain but a withering look from Death quickly shut him up.

"Come on, let's get you upstairs," Holiday smiled, holding out a hand.

Beetle took it and got shakily to his feet. I stood up and wrapped a steadying arm about him. Beetle wasn't very tall for a demon, one of the reasons his brethren shunned him, but he was solidly built and when he swayed backwards, he almost took me with him. That had been happening a lot in the last couple of hours.

Holiday laughed, a deep cheerful sound, and helped me right the demon. Chappie, as usual, did nothing.

"Clean up Brimstone's stall and look to the other horses while Mary Jane is looking after Beetle," Death ordered the sulking stable hand. "Lucifer will expect the stalls to be clean upon his return."

Even I felt the cold malice emanating off the stable hand as Chappie turned wordlessly and went to work, shoulders hunched, jaw grinding.

"I'm going back to the pub," Death announced with a wave of his hand. "See you later, sweetheart."

Death cast Doc Holiday a warning glance. Holiday laughed.

"I don't envy you, Mary Jane," Doc Holiday whispered in my ear as we helped Beetle up the stairs to his bed. "You need better help. Lucifer should send that Aussie back to the pit."

"It's his punishment," I replied hoarsely, the smell of soap, cigars, whiskey, and male musk drifting off Holiday in waves. My knees almost buckled. If Doc Holiday noticed my flushed face and weak knees he was gentleman enough not to remark upon it.

We poured Beetle into his narrow cot and left him there to sleep. I tucked him in, my motherly instinct kicking in. It was quite hilarious considering Beetle was five times my age. Demons matured at a much slower rate than humans.

"I'll leave you some laudanum. Give him four drops for pain as needed," the doc told me, handing me a small bottle with a stopper on it. "These demons aren't fly weights so don't be stingy."

I blushed even redder when my hand brushed his. The doc grinned. Heat burned my cheeks and ears. One might say my toes even curled.

"Good to see you again, Mary Jane," he winked. "Don't be a stranger, drop by the cottage for a drink some time."

"Thanks, I'll do that," I squeaked.

The doc swung around and medical bag in hand sauntered out of the room with a swagger that only a man like Doc Holiday could pull off. It took a few minutes for my heart rate to settle down. I looked at the place on my hand where his hand had touched mine. I fought down the unreasonable urge to never wash that hand again, but Beetle's dried blood stained my skin black.

"I am such a lost cause," I mumbled to the sleeping demon. "If that bed were larger, I'd join you."

A series of long booming horn blasts and the howl of Hell hounds on the hunt rattled the windows. I didn't know if that meant they had caught the bandits or were summoning more de- mons and hounds to the cause. I shivered, wishing the misguided souls who stole the devil's horses luck. They were going to need it.

The Hunt Continues

I lay in bed for hours staring at the wooden beams that criss-crossed the vaulted ceiling. I wanted to cry, but my tears had all dried up. If I had a soul, it would be bruised and weary from the endless snarls and myriad of cursing coming from the sullen army that marched past the stable doors. I dreaded Lucifer and Diana's empty-handed return.

I tried to think of my last ride, at the cheering throngs of people standing on the sidelines watching the riders traverse the event course. There was one man I thought I'd recognized, but it was at the water jump and it took all my focus to keep Leyland from refusing it like he had in the past. I scrunched up my face, trying in vain to envision him. It wasn't a big surprise that my brain refused, especially since that was the jump where I was murdered.

My thoughts turned back to the present. It was obvious the bandits had escaped through the gates Geryon had abandoned in favor of drinks with his crew at The Hoof & Hammer Gentlemen's Club. The *One Hour War* had left Hell unguarded and it was my fault.

My heart was heavy.

The clip-clop of steel shoes on stone echoed through the stable. Stone floors and walls carried the sound. Uncle Lucifer and Diana were back.

I jumped out of bed and raced down the stairs, my mind was racing and my body rebelling.

The horses dragged their feet. Sweat coated their necks and haunches. Charlemagne's head bobbed with exhaustion. Anger replaced the depression that had consumed me over the last five hours. The two deities had ridden the horses hard. Charlemagne was too out of shape to be galloping all over Hell and back at such a furious pace.

Lucifer's face was dark and brooding. Diana hunched over the warhorse's neck, nursing a dislocated shoulder. I silently promised to give Charlemagne an extra heaping of grain when she was gone.

"Take him," Diana snarled, sliding off his back.

The goddess's clothing was covered in dirt and debris. Her sun-kissed hair was wilted and lackluster. I bit back a smile.

"Shall I call Doc Holiday," I asked sweetly.

Diana glared at me, tossed Charlemagne's reins at my face and stalked off to find Doc Holiday, her left shoulder bent forward at an awkward angle.

"Do be more civil to my guests, Mary Jane," Uncle Lucifer grumbled.

"Can't promise anything, but I'll try," I replied brightly.

Lucifer grunted and dismounted. He led Brimstone to the wash rack and painstakingly rubbed the sweat from the stallion's neck with a wet sponge. Brimstone nipped at the sponge, annoyed that the hunt had not been successful.

I removed Charlemagne's bridle, pulled a leather halter over his head, and then tied Charlemagne in front of his stall and began currying him down. The gigantic horse sighed with pleasure and closed his eyes.

"Good boy," I whispered to him, careful to make sure Lucifer was out of earshot. "What a nag that goddess is. I don't like her either."

Charlemagne opened one eye and turned his massive head towards me. He rubbed his ears and forelock against my shoulder. I laughed. Though big and clunky, Charlemagne was as regal as Brimstone in his own way.

"He likes you and in some ways more dangerous than Brimstone," Lucifer chuckled as he placed Brimstone in his stall. "Don't let him dominate you. He can turn in a heartbeat and slam you into the stall and crush you with those monster hooves of his. I lost many a good squire to him over the years. He enjoys killing. Don't ever forget that."

"He can dominate me if he wants," I chuckled, snuggling my face into his mane. "The horses are all I've got now."

Lucifer nodded absently, not really listening to me, and closed the black stallion's stall door. Brimstone drained the water bucket and then began nibbling at his hay.

"I want you to go upside," my uncle said abruptly, joining me at Charlemagne's stall.

"But who will look after the horses with Beetle on bed rest," I gasped. "Chappie's useless, and I thought I couldn't go back to earth. I'm banished, aren't I?"

"I'll make sure the horses are looked after," Lucifer replied tightly, "even if I have to clean the stalls myself."

"But...but," I stammered, at a loss for words.

"If I say you go upside, you go upside," Lucifer spat and then softened. "You are the only one I trust to bring the boys home safely."

Now I really was at a loss as to what to say.

"I'm not a lawman. I don't know how to track down criminals," I stammered, my normal bravado gone with the wind.

What if I failed?

What if I ended up beaten over the head like Beetle?

Maybe I could take Doc Holiday with me?

"I don't think I can do this alone," I confessed, embarrassed.

Where was the fearless event rider and the rebellious Nephilim? Not here evidently.

"Yes, you can, you'll have me and my legions at your service as soon as you find them," Lucifer said, the argument settled. "Don't worry about packing a bag. You can stay with your mother, but you mustn't under any circumstances visit your horse or your girlfriends. Understand? I am your liege lord. I command you to find my horses and bring those four humans back to me to face justice!"

"Yes, uncle," I agreed.

"You are strong. You are invisible!"

"Isn't that a song," I blurted out. I seemed to remember an old song like that. My mother used to sing it. The words sprang into my mind: 'I am strong; I am invincible; I am woman'.

Lucifer shook his head in frustration.

"I said 'invisible', not 'invincible'," he corrected me.

"Oh," I shrugged.

Uncle was right, I was strong. If I could make the Olympic Team, although technically I hadn't quite made it since I had been murdered first, but close is a winner in horseshoes, then I could find the bandits who stole Binky, Mr. Jeepers, Styx and Diablo.

"I got this, uncle," I said, feigning confidence.

"I knew you would," he smiled. "I've already sent word to Geryon to let you pass. When you've captured those fools, or found where they've holed up, send for me first. The hunt is still on. Try not to rock all the realms again when you do it."

"Okay," I nodded sheepishly.

Lucifer spun on his heel and stalked off.

Charlemagne snuffled my hair. I rubbed his nose, stunned to be given such a task by the Prince of Darkness himself; to be trusted so was an honor.

"You'd never stomp on me, would you buddy," I whispered to the Hell horse, "not like that nasty huntress. You can stomp on her anytime."

The warhorse nuzzled me gently.

I led Charlemagne into his stall and took off his halter. I felt much better. For the first time in my life I wasn't ashamed to be who I was. Uncle Lucifer was right; I was strong... and invincible... and a woman.

Wait, what did he say? Invisible? Huh!

"Uncle Luci," I hollered, but it was too late, my uncle was gone.

I stood there lamely wondering what to do. Was I expected to fly out of Hell, walk, or grab one of the other Hell horses and ride out? I had never entered or left Hell without my uncle or my mother by my side. I didn't even know which direction the gates were in.

There was also the matter of my murder. I was officially dead upside. How could I stay with my mother and not be recognized as a dead half-angel walking? What if my murderer was upside and killed me again? If I ended up back at the Pearly Gates, would Saint

Peter send me straight to Purgatory? Death had warned me there was worse things than... well... death.

"This being dead is a real bummer," I told Charlemagne.

The warhorse's legs buckled. He sank onto the bedding in his stall and closed his eyes, tiredness overtaking him. Within seconds he was sound asleep, his bottom lip quivering, his breathing softening into a comforting rumble.

"I'll get you some grain before I leave."

Brimstone nickered softly from his stall.

"Don't worry, I won't forget you," I smiled, my spirits lifting.

Death and Doc Holiday jogged around the corner and skidded to a stop in front of me as I exited the feed room with two buckets of grain, one in each hand.

"Is it true," Death sneered. "Is Lucifer sending you upside to catch those bandits by yourself?"

"Yes," I said, bristling. "He thinks I'm capable, don't you?"

"Mary Jane, this isn't a lark," Doc Holiday replied sternly. "It's dangerous and for some reason, Diana has you in her crosshairs."

"That's because one of her arrows killed me and she wasn't the one to fire it," I replied blithely.

Holiday rolled his eyes at me.

"Look, sweetie, nobody but your mother will be able to see you other than the bandits if they're mounted on the Hell horses," Death said, back pedaling.

"And the witches," Holiday chimed.

"And possibly a few gifted humans," Death added.

"And the undead stuck on earth," Holiday continued.

"Plus any half-deities, half-angels, and Hell spawn working upside to tempt souls," Death croaked. "Mostly though, you will be invisible."

"Ohhhh! That's what my uncle meant," I bleated, feeling like a sacrificial lamb heading to slaughter.

"Lucifer does nothing without an ulterior motive," Doc Holiday cautioned me.

"If you need help, close your eyes and whisper Binky's name," Death stammered. "Binky dotes on you. If you're in trouble, Binky will know it and summon me."

"That goes for Mr. Jeepers," Doc Holiday said. "He belonged to me before he belonged to the Grim Reaper."

"Wait a minute. Are you saying you know where they are?" I gasped, following the logic where it took me. I may have failed math and biology, but I'm no dummy. If what they said was true, Binky and Mr. Jeepers could check in with them.

"No, we don't," Doc Holiday scowled raising his hands in surrender.

"Like I told you before, they're off on an adventure and don't appear to want to be found just yet," Death snorted.

No wonder my uncle was so angry. If Binky and Mr. Jeepers weren't answering Death's or Doc Holiday's calls, then Diablo and Styx weren't answering Lucifer's summons' either. Oh boy, that was some Catch 22.

"Give us the buckets, we'll feed Brimstone and Charlemagne and check on the rest of the horses," Doc Holiday said, reaching for a bucket.

"You need to get going," Death admonished me, tearing one of the buckets out of my hand, "or you'll be in bigger trouble than you already are."

"How," I asked feebly, suddenly feeling ill.

"Shake out those wings of yours and follow the River Styx," Death answered, annoyed with me.

"And remember what we said," Holiday quipped.

How could I forget? Invisibility. Witches. Lost souls. Half-deities. Not likely.

I handed over the last bucket to Doc Holiday and walked briskly out of the barn. I peeled off my jacket and shook out my girls. My purple wings shone with a heavenly light. They were like bright disco balls spinning brightly against the black landscape of Hell as I flexed them. Before I knew it I was off the ground and speeding towards the river.

"Say hello to your mother for me," Doc Holiday shouted behind me.

Good grief, was there any single men in Hell Town that hadn't dated my mother? Ugh.

Gotta Love GPS

My hometown was a big little town with a lot of heart surrounded by farmland and lush meadows of wild flowers. It was an alcove of peace and joy outside of the mainstream world in which chaos ruled… not! I'm just yanking your chain.

Merrickville started out as a single train station at the fork of two major rail lines running west. It was now a massive freight depot that shipped items across the continent and was surrounded by an industrial wasteland. Even after a hundred years, the freight trains ran non-stop. The farmland surrounding it had been eaten up by Walmart, Home Depot, Costco, and countless other big box store warehouses. The population had quadrupled due to the need for more and more warehouse workers. The streets were haphazard, some going north south and others going east west, with dead end cul-de-sacs everywhere, no thought going into city planning as the ever greater needs of the residents overwhelmed the once small town.

Our house was a small two bedroom two-storey affair located two streets over from the sprawling train yard. No matter how hard my mother tried to grow flowers or vegetables in the garden, they always died shortly after sprouting. She had given up long ago and had Astroturf installed in the front yard. Hence, the reason I had taken to spending most of my time growing up either in Hell or at a riding stable fifty-miles west of Merrickville.

As I spread my wings and slowed down over the neighborhood I had grown up in, I welcomed the feeling of coming home. Old lady Meir's cat, Mrs. Butterfield, a ginger longhaired nuisance, glared up at me, her yellow eyes blinking in surprise, a hiss escaping her throat, as she watched me land none too gracefully on the front doorstep.

I hissed back at her and the cat raced under the front porch of her own house, a whitewashed version of our cornflower yellow and rainbow colored window sash one.

"Mom, I'm home," I yelled as I walked into the house.

Our home looked the same as ever. A large navy blue leather couch took up most of the living room, a tight pile wool carpet with grey and white squares covered the pinewood floors in front of it. A yoga mat was rolled up in front of the fireplace and a Pilate's ball rested against the TV stand. The TV stand was covered in herb pots and a stack of books on metaphysics, my mother a firm believer in meditation and all things related to the astral plane. Thankfully, we did have internet which she needed to keep her business going.

The mellow yellow walls were covered with colorful photographs of majestic mountains and roiling oceans with inspirational quotes either in the clouds or beneath the deep blue sea. Of all of them my favorite was the tiny picture of a cat hanging from a pole with a quote underneath the cat that said 'hang in there, baby'. The quote was the story of our lives.

"Mom," I shouted louder. "You home?"

"Don't yell, I'm in the kitchen," she said, walking into the living room cleaning the flour off her hands with a kitchen towel. She greeted me with a wide smile.

"I'm making blueberry pancakes," she grinned, knowing they were my favorite.

At forty-five my mother could have competed in the Miss World Pageant. She was breathtakingly beautiful with sandy colored skin, luxurious curly black hair, deep brown eyes, thick luscious lips, and a body that could launch a hundred battle ships. She looked like a movie starlet from the nineteen forties or fifties. Somehow, I had missed all of that, favoring my great-grandmother instead.

Great Grandma had crossed the continent in a wagon train. She was the definition of pioneer stock: strong, big boned, and capable. Except for the wings and purple hair, I looked just like the image in the antique photo on the mantle over the fireplace.

I rushed over to my mum and wrapped her in a giant bear hug: "How did you know I was coming so soon?"

"Lucifer sent me a message," she laughed, breaking out of the hug and motioning me into the kitchen.

"I see," I chuckled, noticing the enormous bouquet of red roses on the kitchen table, a black note with a cartoon red devil stamped into the upper right corner of it. "I didn't know they had Fed-Ex delivery in Hell."

"Oh, yes, they do," my mom said happily, dropping a spoonful of batter onto the griddle.

I wonder if Diana knew about my mother and Lucifer's... er, friendship?

My brow furrowed when I looked around the kitchen.

Where were the flowers and sympathy cards?

I mean I only died yesterday. One would think someone would have noticed.

My mother hummed as she made breakfast. I didn't recognize the tune.

"Mum, how come there aren't any cards or flowers," I asked, unable to help myself.

"Oh, I threw them out," she said. "The flowers died days ago."

"But I only died yesterday," I replied, stunned.

"Oh, dear, no, you were murdered over two months ago," she answered, depositing three perfectly round blueberry buckwheat pancakes on a plate and handing it to me.

I inhaled sharply. I'd been dead for over two months. That was a bit of a shock to the system.

"You'll be happy to know that I gave Leyland away to your old coach for her daughter to ride. They're so cute together. Melissa is only ten, but she rides him everywhere. Leyland's a real trooper and looks after her," my mother gushed as she sat down at the table with just one pancake and a cup of fruit. "Linda promised me Leyland would have a forever home."

I sighed with relief. If Linda promised Leyland a forever home then he would have one.

"Babs and Bernie call me every week to see how I'm doing or if I need anything. Bernie has decided to go off to college and study nursing. Babs still works at the stable. She's like you, a horse nut for life. They are so sweet. Of course, Lucifer told me I can't tell them anything about you."

"Huh," I mused, digging into a pancake. I still hadn't gotten over the fact that I'd been dead for two months when it only felt like twenty-four hours. That was Hell time for you.

"So what about my murder," I asked. "Have they found out who killed me yet?"

"No, but Detective Smith is on it," she chirped, cutting her pancake into long thin diagonals. "He checks in regularly. At first, he suspected Sandy, the red-haired girl with the cute little bob and boob job that's always sticking her tongue out at you behind your back. I thought she'd have grown out of that habit by now. Did you know she had it in for you? I mean, she's rude, yes, but shooting you with an arrow? I sure didn't see that one coming. It ended up it wasn't her, she had a solid alibi. She took your spot on the Olympic Team though."

"Yeah, Sandy's a piece of work. She was always looking down her nose at me and Leyland. Let me guess, her alibi was Jimmy Brady. He's a cheating twit, I should know," I replied glumly. "Still, she is capable of throwing daggers, but you're right, only with her eyes and tongue. She doesn't have the courage to kill anyone."

Mom gave me the look that said she didn't approve of my negative energy.

"What about this detective? Is he single?"

"No, he has a wife and four kids," my mother laughed, knowing where I was going with that question. "So, why are you up here? Your uncle didn't tell me."

"He sent me upside to retrieve his horses," I mumbled, savoring the last chunk of pancake in my mouth. "Four guys stole them. They even took Binky and Mr. Jeepers. Geryon left the gates open when he went partying."

"How on earth are they going to keep Binky a secret," she cried, almost choking on a teeny weensy piece of pint sized pancake.

"And poor Geryon, he must be devastated."

"I'm sure he is," I winced, deciding not to tell her about the *One Hour War* my death caused and the resulting celebrations. "You're right though. I don't see how they can hide a walking skeletal Hell horse."

"People will think they're seeing a ghost rider or being put on," she said thoughtfully. "Perhaps you should go on YouTube or Vimeo and see if anyone's posted any videos."

"You know mum you're positively brilliant at times," I grinned.

"Of course I am, I'm your mother," she quipped, pushing away from the table.

"I guess you're working this morning," I chuckled, picking up my plate and hers and taking them over to the sink to wash.

"I'm afraid I am," she said, giving me a quick peck on the cheek. "I have three classes back-to-back, a spin class, and a yoga class for beginners, plus a meditation work shop late this afternoon. I wish I could stay, but I have a mortgage to pay and no daughter to help me do it anymore."

"S'okay, mum, go do your thing and I'll go see what I can find out," I smiled. "Maybe once I find the horse thieves I can ask uncle about a finder's fee. I'll give it you to help out."

"Thank you, sweetheart, but I can manage. I might be late for dinner so help yourself to what's in the fridge. Your cell phone is in your desk drawer. I kept up the payments. I had a feeling you'd be back," she said before planting another quick kiss on my cheek and sweeping out of the room in a flurry of hair and lavender and sage. She always cleaned her chakras with lavender and sage before heading to her fitness studio. I expected that was where I got the idea to color my hair and wings purple from.

I made myself a cup of English breakfast tea, my mother not allowing coffee in the house even if it was a fair trade brand, and headed to my room. That was her idea of being a conscientious objector. No argument on my part could dissuade her from her views on the wickedness of cocoa and caffeine. I thought living in a house by a train depot, a place where even weeds didn't grow, was a lot nastier than chocolate or coffee, but there weren't a lot of places a single mother could afford to live and support herself and her horse crazy daughter in Merrickville. You know what they say, home is where the heart is, and this place was where mine was.

The smell of Leyland greeted me as I opened my bedroom door and saw my show jacket, breeches and riding boots tucked inside the corner of my closet. The rest of the room was as I left it – a total mess.

I turned on my computer and opened up a browser. I typed the words 'ghost rider videos' into the search bar and waited. Over forty videos popped up on the screen including movie trailers, cast interviews, Nicolas Cage sightings, but there were also numerous accounts of ghost rider sightings and even a news story about a crazy bank robbery by a group of cowboys. The newer stories and videos took place over the last three weeks.

I clicked on the bank robbery video.

"Oh, oh, Lucifer is going to flip," I grimaced as I watched the shaky black and white video of four men dressed in old West regalia complete with cowboy hats, leather slickers, six guns, spurs, and bandanas, galloping three hellfire breathing horses and one lively boney steed through the broken window of a bank carrying bags of loot. The film was traffic camera quality.

I had to admit, the robbery made my heart race. It was darned sexy the way they cavalierly robbed the bank. The comments under the videos were mostly from women agreeing with my opinion.

There wasn't just one video like this but at least ten, plus eyewitness accounts of being robbed by what the news reports were calling the *Ghost Rider Gang*. One woman fanned herself with her check book, her face flushed, eyes dreamily fixed upon a point over top of the camera as she described willingly giving her engagement ring and cash to one of the four bandits on horseback. She said they were all very polite and quite charming, but the bandit she gave her ring to had 'bedroom eyes'.

I watched all of the bank robbery videos. The horses looked like they were having the time of their lives. I knew those horses well. They kicked out with glee when they crashed through the bank windows. Death and Doc Holiday were right. The horses went willingly. I doubted the *Ghost Rider Gang* had a clue as to how intelligent the horses really were or what the consequences would be when the devil caught up with them.

That gave me an idea. I pulled out a virtual map and placed pins in the location of each bank robbery and then marked off the reported sightings of a bone horse. The bone horse sightings were less frequent and formed a cluster around Denver, Colorado, while the bank robberies were farther afield in smaller towns with less police resources. Denver was as good a place as any to start.

Maybe I was a natural detective? Perhaps I should have gone into law enforcement instead of focusing on a professional riding career? Maybe I'd still be alive if I did.

I gulped down my tea, retrieved my cell phone from my desk drawer, and powered up my wings.

Okay, I basically walked out the front door and flew away, but it sounds better to say I powered up my wings like I was a Marvel super hero. I also needed the GPS on my phone to locate Denver. Like I said before, I had to keep my wings battened down unless I was in Hell. I had no idea which direction was which. Without the GPS, I could have wound up in Antarctica.

"Ya gotta love GPS," I grinned as the lady stated: "Turn right on Interstate 15 and continue north".

Binky

I sat on a bench overlooking one of the lakes in the Denver City Park. It was still early morning on a week day so there weren't a lot of people around. It was a shame because it was a beautiful day. The lake was still, the barest of breezes rippling the water. The sun warmed my face.

"Sorry, guys, I'm travelling light," I told the two Canada Geese eyeing me hopefully. I guess birds could see me too.

I turned my attention back to Google maps. The last video of Binky and his rider walking along the summit of a mountain trail was close to Eldorado Springs. I knew there would be no cell reception in that area so I studied the aerial maps and tried to match them up with the video.

The video was shot by an ecstatic hiker two days ago. While Binky's rider wasn't wearing a mask, he rode far enough away that all I could tell was that he had dirty blond hair, broad shoulders, and was an experienced rider. He rode with ease. The saddle on Binky's back looked worn and comfortable. That was about it. Not much to go on, but the location the hiker pinged was far from civilization, at the top of a trailhead that disappeared down a steep rocky path leading to one of the popular white water rafting rivers.

"Time to go hunt me down some varmints," I said to the geese as a woman walked by with a stroller. The two red-headed twins inside looked right at me. I waggled my fingers at them and spread my wings to show them I was just a happy, harmless half-angel. One of the twins, the farthest away from me giggled with glee; the other one screamed blue murder.

"Jeremy, what's got into you," the twins' mother yelped. "Don't worry, those geese won't hurt you, they're just looking for a hand-out."

The geese honked and waddled back to the water.

I smothered a laugh as I rose a few feet into the air, sticking out my tongue and making a funny face at the kids. The smiling twin giggled so hard he blew a spit bubble. Jeremy, the very unhappy twin, howled like a dog in an earthquake.

I laughed even harder and shot straight up into the air like a cannon ball blasted off the bow of a Spanish galleon.

The sun was brighter above the smattering of clouds; I squinted to see where I was going. I had a vague idea of direction and pocketed my cell phone as I left the city in the mountains behind. The air tasted sweet and clean.

I flew over several bounteous parks with lakes and creeks and trailheads zigzagging through quaking forests of aspen and tall fir. Modern subdivisions marred the landscape between the vast open ranges with giant houses on postage stamped lots. I could envision what this land must have looked like when the first settlers came. Even with all the new developments, my mother would love it here. She could grow grass.

I caught a strong air current and glided north by northwest through the Rocky Flats Wildlife Preserve. I tucked my wings tightly against my body and dove down towards the Historic Lindsay Ranch buildings, skimming the top of the grasslands between the elegant white windmills that dotted the hillside. It felt glorious to simply fly and just 'be' without worrying about being seen. My heart soared as I dipped and dived, doing full roll-overs in the air above the plains.

For over an hour I forgot about the fact that I was dead and on the hunt for a gang of horse thieves until I was flying upside down, my hair streaming out behind me, and the most gorgeous hunk-a-hunk-a burning love rode Binky out of the tree-line his eyes riveted on my death defying aerial show. That was when I flew head first into a fir tree and landed upside down in a heap at the base of the very 'same' tree.

Mr. Studley trotted the skeletal horse, equine bones rattling, spurs jingling, over to where I lay with my boots in the air, my wings splayed in two separate directions, my neck craned sideways, and bum resting against the tree trunk. It was the most unladylike pose I'd ever been caught in and that took into account the debaucheries Death and I got into during a pub crawl on my twenty-first birthday.

"Hello," I said meekly, turning my head to try to look at him right side up.

"Hello," Mr. Studley of the sea blue eyes, rakish blond hair, tanned face, strong jaw line and dimpled chin, said. "Are you okay?"

"I think so," I winced, reaching out to straighten my wings before somersaulting backwards into a sitting position.

Mr. Studley was about to dismount, when I stopped him rather bluntly, right leg in mid-air.

"Stop! Don't do that," I snapped.

"Why," he asked, swinging his right leg back over Binky's back.

Binky's left eye socket regarded me. If he had lips, I knew he'd be laughing.

"It's not funny, Binky," I said, rolling my eyes.

Binky threw his head up into the air and nodded several times.

"Are you talking to him," Mr. Studley asked, "or is he talking to you?"

"Both," I blathered on, getting shakily to my feet. Mr. Studley looked oddly familiar, but I couldn't quite place him.

"Are you an angel," he asked, a crooked smile sweeping across his chiseled good looks.

"Maybe," I shrugged.

"The wings are a bit of a giveaway, although the color is a bit odd, isn't it?"

I raised an eyebrow. Now was not the time to explain to him I was only half an angel or that if he dismounted he wouldn't be able to see me at all, nor why I had lavender wings.

"You don't seem surprised to meet an angel?"

"And you don't seem surprised to meet a man riding a skeleton horse," he countered.

I folded my arms across my chest and blew a stray strand of purple hair out of my face.

"My name's Lucas by the way," he said, reaching a hand out towards me.

"Mary Jane," I replied, rubbing my dirty hands on my jeans before standing up and shaking his hand. It was the polite thing to do.

"I know," he grinned.

I don't know what I expected from the bandits known as the *Ghost Rider Gang*, but it wasn't this handsome cowboy with a soft pleasant voice.

"You know my name?" I started, surprised.

"Mary Jane Bligh, international event rider," he said. "It's an honor to meet you. I've been following your career for awhile. You're fearless in the saddle. I managed to catch you ride in three competitions in Virginia this year. That horse of yours put the others to shame in the dressage and cross-country section."

"Thanks," I replied, not knowing what else to say. Mr. Studley knew who I was. Wowsers!

"Have you always had wings or did you get them after you died?"

"That's a very personal question," I snapped.

"Sorry, curiosity got the better of me. I was there when you were killed, off on the sidelines. You sure managed to get Leyland over his fear of water though. He finished the jump even though you fell off in the middle of it and went splashing into the water with an arrow sticking out of your chest."

I went mute. I didn't know what to say to that, and then it hit me; he was the guy I noticed before my life changed forever, the dude on the sidelines that I'd picked out of the crowd.

Was he a stalker?

Maybe I'd better be careful. Then again, maybe he saw who killed me?

Instead, I said: "You're in trouble, Binky," and wagged my finger at the Hell horse. I really should be hollering for my uncle, but I wasn't ready yet. "Death misses you and Uncle Lucifer is furious."

The cowboy called Lucas blushed.

"Don't be mad at Binky," he croaked, his brows knitting together in a totally adorable scowl. "This whole thing was my brother's idea."

"How so," I asked, my own cheeks burning.

Binky head-butted me in the chest.

I laughed throatily. I took my first riding lesson on Binky. Death was ever so patient, even when I tried to gallop off into a particularly glorious sunset across the Hellfire plains. I broke my tailbone when I fell off. I've broken it a half dozen times since then.

"Me, my brother, and a couple of buddies were vacationing in Hawaii. I swear my brother, Elijah, and I had gone mad. A battle right out of a Hollywood blockbuster raged above the Kīlauea volcano. What was supposed to be a once in a lifetime vacation in Hawaii had turned into a real life Armageddon. I thought we were all gonna die.

The sky lit up like New Year's Eve. Bombs of molten lava exploded all around us. Thunder boomed and metal twanged as swords clashed, winged angels and hellish winged demons collided in midair."

My body started to tremble. Lucas was describing the *One Hour War*. He had witnessed it. It never dawned on me how many people on Earth might have seen my downfall and the repercussions of summoning my Uncle Lucifer.

"Run! Elijah screamed, grabbing me by the arm and pulling me towards a lava tube to the right as a hail of red hot lava rained down on us," Lucas continued. "Caleb and Ronin followed on our heels. My brother was always reckless and climbed straddle-legged to the top of the lava tube, back to the wall, until he was able to watch what was going on from the sheltered lip of the rock tube without getting burned alive by the still flying lava. Man, my lungs felt like I had swallowed battery acid."

"Is that how you got the sword and armor," I interrupted him. "Beetle said one of you was wearing heavenly armor and carrying an angel's sword. They aren't hard to miss. They glow in the dark."

"Let me finish," Lucas scolded me.

"Fine," I said, annoyed. I held up my hands in supplication. "Sorry."

"Elijah shouted down to us that he could see Hell and where the demons were coming from. I didn't believe it so I climbed up the tube and looked out. Sure enough, there were the flames of Hell and squadrons of flying demons coming out of this deep pit. There were demons and angels fighting in the sky above us. Below us was a river, plains, and I swear I could see a whole town."

I stamped one foot, impatient that he wasn't answering my question: where did he get the sword?

"There was this ear-splitting sonic boom as a black angel with massive wings and a tiny purple angel fell at lightning speed through the clouds towards the opening to Hell, the winged demons parting and then closing protectively around them as they plummeted into the volcano's mouth," Lucas stopped, taking a breath. "Wait, was that purple angel you?"

"Maybe," I cringed.

"So, you're from Hell and not Heaven?"

"Skip to the part about how you got the sword and armor, and maybe I'll tell you more," I growled, placing my hands on my hips.

"Yeah, well, an angel fell to the ground close to where we were hiding and Elijah ran out and grabbed his sword. Since he looked like he was dead, he stole his chain mail too," Lucas sighed, his face reddening. "The next thing I knew Elijah convinced us all to sneak into Hell to look around, figuring he could protect us with the sword and armor. You can imagine our surprise when we stumbled upon these giant unmanned iron gates and a stable filled with the most gorgeous horses we had ever seen. I mean, the sight of those horses made my knees buckle, you know what I mean? All we could think of was breeding those stallions to regular mares. We'd end up with some of the finest bloodstock in the world. It was a dream come true."

"So, you thought stealing four Hell horses and laying a beating on a poor kid would make your dreams come true," I rounded on him, anger consuming me for Beetle's sake. "Oh, wait, you didn't try to breed a skeleton horse to a live mare, which is impossible by the way, or breed any of the other stallions either, you decided to rob not one, not two, but ten banks instead."

"Kid? That monster was just a kid," Lucas paled. "He almost ripped Caleb's arm off?"

"In demon terms, yes, Beetle is just a teenager," I barked.

"We didn't know," Lucas apologized. "Elijah hit him with the blunt end of the sword. We thought he was going to kill Caleb."

"Yeah, well your bro almost killed my friend," I spat.

"Really, I'm sorry," Lucas cried. "I hope he's okay?"

I softened a bit. It was clear Lucas was devastated to find out Beetle was nothing more than a teenager. At least it wasn't Lucas who had hurt him. That would have been a bummer because Lucas was pretty darned cute and the magnetic tug to... I don't know... leap into his arms and rip his shirt off, was pretty overwhelming.

Have I lost my mind?

I decided to chalk my carnal thoughts to the stress of the last few day, or months, according to my mom. The afterlife was getting complicated.

I stared down at my hands for a moment, thinking over how to proceed.

"Lucifer is my uncle. Binky belongs to Death, one of the Four Horsemen," I said after the uncomfortable silence that had ensued. "Mr. Jeepers is the light dappled grey. He used to belong to Doc Holiday, but when Doc died and went to Hell, Mr. Jeepers wanted to follow him. Doc ended up giving him to the Grim Reaper so Jeepers had something to do. Death, Doc Holiday and the Grim Reaper, at least the reaper that rides Mr. Jeepers, are a good lot, but Styx and Diablo are my uncle's mounts. My uncle is not a fan of yours."

"I see," Lucas said, sidestepping the Hell horse closer to me. He then folded his arms across the saddle horn and leaned forward. His warmth breath tickled my nostrils as I stared up into those twin pools of heavenly delight. His breath smelled of bacon, toast and scrambled eggs, my new favorite breakfast.

My heart went pitter-patter.

This wasn't good. We shouldn't be chitchatting. I shouldn't be mooning over a horse thief. I should be summoning my uncle and all the demons in Hell.

I absently reached around and plucked fir needles out of my feathers, breaking eye contact, and trying to decide what to do as my feelings for this man intensified. I mean, I wasn't some doe-eyed teenager. I was a grown woman with a mission to fulfill. There was no time for dilly-dallying.

What was happening to me?

"Lucas," someone shouted from deep inside the forest. It was a loud masculine voice.

I exhaled sharply.

"Perhaps we can talk again some time," he grinned. "I have to go."

"You can't," I replied, my voice cracking.

Oh by all the deities above and below but he had a beautiful smile.

"I don't think Binky wants to go back to Hell with you," he chuckled, mistaking my stopping him for my being responsible and doing my job. "You're going to have to come up with something better than simply chastising him."

Ugh, he did know how smart the Hell horses were. I glared at Binky – the traitor. I swear the Hell horse winked at me even though he only had twin black holes beneath the gaping bone eye sockets.

"You're sure you'll be okay," he asked, circling Binky around me.

"I'll live," I hissed, "sort of."

I folded my arms around my body as shivers rippled up and down my arms. I felt like a drowning sailor, except I wasn't drowning and I wasn't cold.

"Sure?"

"Sure," I barked, aggravated.

So much for the element of surprise! Uncle Lucifer was going to be furious when he found out I located two of the bandits and didn't summon him. Of course, if I didn't tell him about it, he wouldn't be the wiser for it.

Lucas reined Binky in. The bone horse reared. He backed the

horse up and like a circus performer, leaned over to whisper in my ear: "I feel it too." He then righted himself and galloped off into the forest after whoever had called him.

A gamut of emotions ran through me including anger, fear, confusion, and gut wrenching-still-my-beating-heart-throw-caution-to-the-wind desire as I watched him disappear into the forest.

The horse thief mesmerized me. Finally, I shook out my wings, making sure nothing was broken, before lifting off and flying to the fire tower atop the mountain in the distance. I hoped from there I could see where Lucas and his companion were headed.

The next time, I vowed to be more prepared and wouldn't allow him to get so up close and personal.

Yeah, who was I kidding?

Sweet Desire

I sat atop the fire tower munching on a chicken burger for a long time watching Lucas and his companion make their way down the mountain trail to the river below. I had liberated the burger from a cook in a diner off the interstate. The poor guy had gone apoplectic on turning to see the burger gone from the plate he had just placed it on. He accused the second cook of stealing it. The second cook threw a hissy fit and threw a bowl of salad in the other cook's face. A food fight of righteous proportions ensued.

I know, I am such a pest. It was hilarious though and nobody knew who stole the burger. Invisibility had its perks. It was an excellent burger by the way. The crust was extra crispy, the chicken moist, and the bun was a top shelf bakery Calabrese delight.

I smacked my lips together as I watched Styx lead the way down the mountain and through the river to a side tributary channel. Styx was a flashy buckskin mustang. Lucifer commandeered Styx from Billy the Kid after Billy's friend, Pete Maxwell, shot him dead in Fort Sumner, New Mexico, all because Billy had the late night munchies and wanted a snack. Death had a warped sense of humor that day.

Billy now works as a sheriff in Hell Town alongside the Earp brothers. What can I say; my uncle is a fan of the old West gangsters. Personally, I think Billy the Kid is a toad.

The fire tower I sat upon wasn't manned by a human so I wasn't disturbing anyone. Butterflies tickled my stomach walls like fireflies knocking against the sides of a glass jar. Lucas swayed seductively in the saddle in time with Binky's steps. Sweat beaded my upper lip. Being a half-angel gave me extraordinary eyesight and I took advantage of it; although, I felt a bit like a peeping Tom.

"I'm too sexy for my horse, too sexy for my hat, too sexy," I sang between burger bites.

The cowboy aboard Styx looked so much like Lucas that he had to be Lucas' brother. He had a mean set to his mouth though. Lucas' face was open and warm. Even now, Lucas rode with a slight smile on his lips. Perhaps he was thinking of me? I liked to think so because I was sure thinking of him. I reminded myself that his brother had brutally beaten Beetle and Lucas hadn't stopped him. Apology or not, Lucas' inaction in the face of injustice was a strike against him no matter what my libido was telling me.

So, was it love at first sight or was I 'hot to trot' as Death would say? My heart said it was the first, my brain told me it was the latter, and my body asked what the problem was.

The two bandits disappeared into a patch of cattails and pussy willows bordering the creek tributary. I thought of taking flight to follow them more closely but so long as they were mounted on the Hell horses they could see me.

I was still mulling over the problem when I noticed a puff of smoke rising from the chimney of a small cabin in a meadow at the outer reaches of my angel vision.

I chewed on my lower lip.

Was that where they were going? Was the cabin in the distance their hideout? I needed to know. Other needs burned inside me too, but I squashed those down like a mosquito on my arm.

Nerves raw, I launched off the roof of the squat abandoned fire tower. The wind was warm as it caressed my wings. The sun was a brilliant round ball, blindingly bright. There was something odd about the way the sun hit the top of the trees as I flew over them, and then it hit me, I didn't have a shadow. A tear fell from my eye. It brought home the fact I really was a ghost in this world now.

I banked over the creek at the last point I saw Lucas and his brother, preferring to skim over the tree tops so that I had more cover. I flew a wide circle around the cabin and came in the back way so as not to be seen by the bandits on the Hell horses.

I braked to a stop and ducked inside a tall aspen tree close to the house, grabbing a branch, and slithering beneath the canopy, carefully seeking a perch that would shield my presence but also allow me to watch what the horse thieves were up to.

Lucas and his brother beat me there. The Hell horses were faster than normal horses so it didn't surprise me that Binky and Styx were already unsaddled and turned out with Mr. Jeepers and Diablo, their saddles thrown over the split rail fence close to the cabin. Poor Binky looked lost and forlorn as he stared longingly at the luscious grasses his buddies were happily munching away on.

The smell of wood smoke tickled my nostrils, the smoke curling through the meadow like a tabby cat. I squeezed my nostrils together, fighting back a sneeze. The sneeze built up to foghorn proportions. My loud honk startled the horses. The Hell horses looked up. Diablo, Brimstone's brother, and Mr. Jeepers whinnied a greeting.

"No, no, no," I raised a finger to my lips, trying to shush them.

Lucas and a third man stepped out of the cabin onto the front porch. The third man was a short chestnut haired fellow with tanned skin, brooding grey eyes, and a sour countenance. He looked about twenty-four, but he had school-of-hard-knocks stamped in his features and might have been younger.

"What's got into them, you figure," he grumbled.

Lucas followed the horses' gaze to my hiding spot in the tree and grinned. Even from this far, I could see the twinkle in his eye. My heart went pitter-pat and my stomach flip-flopped.

He couldn't see me – right?

"It's nothing," Lucas replied quietly. "They'd be snorting and pawing if someone was around."

The scowling man grunted and surveyed the horses. Thankfully the herd had gone back to grazing. Seemingly satisfied, he stalked back into the house.

Lucas' lips moved. I could just make out what he said: "I know you're out there."

'I am' I wanted to scream, but didn't. He wouldn't have heard me, but old habits die hard. I didn't want to startle the horses either so I remained silent.

Lucas backed towards the door and finally turned and disappeared into the cabin.

It was dark before I realized I may as well fly home and spend some time with my mother. My back hurt. My legs were cramped. It didn't appear as though the men were going anywhere, plus the other thing I discovered was that mosquitoes could see me too. I swatted at them as they mercilessly tried to drain me dry. What was it I thought about my libido earlier – squash it like a mosquito on my arm – yeah, the goddess of comedy heard me. Payback itched. These new rules of the Universe I had to abide by were strange indeed.

I slowly climbed down the tree and walked over to the horses.

"You guys are bad, you know that," I admonished them.

Each of the horses nuzzled me in turn. I laughed lightly and scratched them under their chins. Only Mr. Jeepers seemed contrite.

"Death and Doc Holiday are really worried about you two," I told Binky and Mr. Jeepers.

"And you guys," I smirked, rubbing a hand down Styx and Diablo's necks, "I know Lucifer has been ignoring you, but running away with a bunch of humans and busting through windows into banks is a little bit over the top, don't you think?"

Styx playfully nipped at my wing feathers and Diablo pinned back his ears. He pawed the earth in irritation.

"Don't be mad at me," I snapped at the black horse. "I have to answer to Lucifer too, but I promise I will put in a good word. I agree with you, Lucifer needs to spend more time with all of you, not dallying with that nasty huntress."

Diablo softened and rubbed his head against my leg. I wrapped my arms around his neck and kissed him.

The door opened and Lucas wandered out onto the porch a can of Budweiser in his hand.

"Where you going," someone called from inside the cabin.

"To check on the horses," Lucas called back.

Lucas took a swig of beer and then placed the can on a wood table beside the door. The table was made of intertwining willow branches. It didn't look like it could hold anymore than one can of beer.

"I know you're out here," he whispered, ambling across the yard and climbing over the fence rail. "You can show yourself. It's not like I haven't seen you already."

"You can't unless you get on a horse," I said throatily, breaking into a mild sweat.

Lucas didn't respond.

Well, this was yet another conundrum in my adventurous new life. I could hear him; he couldn't hear me. Mosquitoes - 1; angel - 0.

I stood still, one hand on Diablo's neck, admiring the fine cut of the cowboy's figure, his strong arms, broad shoulders, narrow hips, and the thin lipped smile that seemed to be his trademark look. I wanted to reach up and run my fingers through his shaggy mop of dark blond hair and feel the taste of his lips on mine.

Oh, I was in way over my head!

On impulse I stepped forward and leaned in to kiss him stopping with my lips a mere inch from his.

"You're close, I can sense you," he said throatily.

Mr. Jeepers knocked me the rest of the way into Lucas' broad chest, my lips locking onto his, while at the same time Binky lowered his head over the cowboy's shoulder.

Lucas's eyes went wide as I suddenly appeared, my lips locked to his. He took it all in stride and kissed me for some time.

Yep, Purgatory here I come.

"Did these horses just set us up," he asked huskily, pulling away.

"They did," I whimpered, every fiber of my being trembling.

"What the heck is that," a gravelly voice swore.

Binky spun around breaking contact with Lucas. Lucas stepped back, puzzled. To him I must have vanished into thin air.

A shot rang out, and then another and another!

Betrayed

"Stop," Lucas screamed too late.

A bullet clipped my wing. Another pierced my shoulder. I wailed in pain as I stumbled away from Lucas, falling to the ground and covering my head with my arms.

I didn't want to die a second time.

I didn't want to call to Lucifer for help again either. The repercussions against me could be catastrophic. Purgatory was worse than Hell. It was a grey limbo where restless spirits never moved on. An eternity there would be worse than oblivion.

The Hell horses went wild and raced to my defense. Binky reared. Mr. Jeepers leapt over the fence and charged the three men on the porch. Diablo and Styx galloped towards me, sliding to a stop, grass and dirt flying, clods of it hitting me in the face, as I lay huddled on the ground, placing themselves between me and the flying bullets.

"I swear to God I just saw a purple haired, purple winged monster kissing Lucas," the chestnut haired man with the cold grey eyes hollered as the other two horse thieves raced outside, guns drawn.

"Holster your guns," Lucas yelled. "She's an angel. If you harmed her, I swear, Ronin, I will never forgive you."

"Are you kidding me, bro," Lucas' brother, Elijah, said, holstering his Colt and advancing on the rearing Hell horse. "Whoa, Mr. Jeepers, take it easy, relax."

"It seems everyone's a little frisky tonight," Caleb joked, his face breaking into a wide grin. "Lucas is getting a little angel action, Jeepers' is getting protective."

Lucas glared at his brother and the other two men on the porch, his teeth grinding in anger. If my wing and shoulder didn't hurt so badly, I'd be flattered by his chivalry, but how was I going to get help without calling Lucifer?

"Mary Jane," Lucas shouted. "Are you okay?"

I could have dragged myself onto Styx or Diablo's back, but my instincts told me that would be a bad move. I was sure the man called Ronin would shoot me double-dead. I could be wrong, but the look in his eye told me I wasn't.

I may not be able to die twice as Death had indicated, but I didn't want to find out so I remained mute and unseen.

Mr. Jeepers quieted down.

Binky stood beside Lucas, gaping eyes staring off into space. Not for the first time, I wondered if Hell horses could get dementia. Binky was really out of sorts.

I held my bleeding arm tightly against my breast and stayed low to the ground. Styx and Diablo continued to stand guard over me. Hopefully the men would go back into the cabin and leave me alone to figure out what to do.

"So," Caleb continued. "Are you holding out on us? Did some hot babe with purple wings fall out of the sky like the dude Elijah stole the sword and chainmail from? Did she bring a girlfriend with her?"

"That wasn't a hot babe," Ronin spat. "You guys didn't see her. She was Barney the dinosaur with wings."

Resentment simmered inside my breast. If I wasn't nursing a busted wing and dripping blood from the bullet hole in my shoulder, I'd sock that guy in the mouth. I know I'm not pretty, but I'm not a purple dinosaur.

Lucas leapt onto the porch and grabbed Ronin by the scruff of his shirt. Fists were raised.

"That's enough, Ronin," Elijah cried, grabbing his brother's arm and spinning him away from the other man.

"Yeah, cool it, buddy," Caleb agreed, pulling Ronin away. "Beauty's in the eye of the beholder, you know what I'm saying. If Lucas has got an angel on the side, who are we to argue. I mean, my whole perception of the universe has changed. There really is a

Hell and a Heaven. We've been to Hell."

Tears pooled in my eyes. I hadn't cried since third grade. Instinctively, I took a liking to the bandit named Caleb. He had curly brown hair with soft features and laugh lines around his eyes. We had never met, yet here he was sticking up for me.

"Well, she's gone now," Elijah reasoned. "Probably flew back to Heaven."

If he only knew, I snorted.

"Way you go, Jeepers," Lucas sighed, opening a gate for the grey to return to the pasture.

The three bandits returned to what they were doing inside the cabin. Lucas closed the gate and then dragged his feet across the yard, head down. He looked over his shoulder, searching the darkness for me, before following after his brother and friends. He closed the door to the cabin with a heart wrenching thump.

I took a deep breath and staggered to my feet. Styx and Diablo snuffled me, concerned.

"I'll be okay, guys," I soothed them. "Thanks for helping me out. You were ever so brave."

Diablo and Styx nodded their heads. They brushed their lips across the top of my head in a gentle kiss. I could smell sweet grass on their breath.

My head felt light. I staggered to my feet and wobbled the few steps towards the tall aspen tree I had been hiding in. Mr. Jeepers trotted over to me. I grabbed a fistful of his mane before I toppled over.

With Diablo flanking me on my right side and Mr. Jeepers on the left I made my way to the tree and sat down with my back against the moss covered bark.

"I know you guys don't want to, but I need one of you to go get Death or Doc Holiday," I said to the three Hell horses. Binky had zoned out by the cabin. I suspected he had a crush on the handsome Lucas too or there was something terminally wrong with him. I didn't even want to consider that option. I made a mental note to ask Doc Holiday about it when I had time.

Mr. Jeepers sniffed my wound and whickered softly.

"Will you do it, my friend," I asked the dappled grey stallion. "Don't bring Uncle Lucifer, just Death or the doc."

Mr. Jeepers placed his downy muzzle against my cheek and let out a long sigh.

"Thank you, Jeeps," I sniffled, feeling drained.

Mr. Jeepers backed away. I heard more than saw him gallop off into the darkness and disappear into the night as the smell of brimstone drifted towards me through the portal to Hell he had opened.

I lay there for some time drifting in and out of consciousness. I stared up through the foliage. The Milky Way was beautiful. It was like a ribbon of Christmas lights had been stretched across the sky. The moon was half-full. Bats flitted back and forth above the grasses. An owl hooted, hunting mice in the dark. Eventually, I closed my eyes and let my mind drift.

"Aren't you a sorry sight," a guttural voice taunted me as the foul stench of sulfur hit me in the face.

My eyes flew open and I beheld the ugliest face in the known universe – King Zagan!

He stood looking down at me, his wings folded back behind him, his horns tipped with gold as were his claws, his expression one of bitter distaste.

"Your majesty, please let me through," Doc Holiday asked politely.

The King grunted and stepped aside to reveal the worried face of Doc Holiday with his leather medical bag swinging back and forth in one hand. I saw Death sitting astride Mr. Jeepers behind him. Death slipped off the horse and raced to my other side. I had never been so glad to see Death, Doc Holiday, and even King Zagan, in all my life, although, I had no idea why the king was here. At least it wasn't my uncle.

"That ruddy centaur wouldn't let us pass without authorization from someone in power," Death explained seeing the questioning look on my face. "Like I need his permission?"

"King Zagan graciously offered to escort us," Doc added, bowing respectfully to the king before kneeling beside me to examine my wounds.

"All hail the wounded hero it seems," King Zagan smirked. "I don't know why Lucifer would send you out without an escort. I would have been happy to have sent one of my generals to find the scum who stole four of Hell's prized horses."

"I don't think my uncle wanted another war just yet," I smiled sweetly, "or for any more shows of force."

King Zagan glared at me. The king always had ulterior motives. I was quite sure he did now as well.

"Agh, your uncle has become weak," Zagan growled. "He can't even control his own mounts. Look at them! They should be patrolling Hell with mine or Duke Zepar's generals aboard them instead of hanging out with humans. You think there hasn't been talk?"

It was hard to argue the king's point. Styx and Diablo grazed in the meadow now that my rescuers had arrived. Mr. Jeepers had already trotted back to join the others and Binky had conveniently melted into the shadows somewhere.

Had Lucifer lost control? Was there a revolt brewing as the king's words implied?

"Let's not spread gossip right now," Doc Holiday interrupted. "I need to manipulate the minor phalanges in your wing back into place. It's going to hurt, Mary Jane. Thankfully the bullet only grazed the bone, but it dislodged four of the smaller phalanges. You aren't going to be able to fly for several days, especially while upside. Angels are fast healing, but you aren't."

King Zagan once again eyed me with disdain.

"What about my shoulder," I asked weakly.

"The bullet went through and through," the doc nodded. "You're lucky. I'll wrap your arm in a sling for formality's sake, but the wound itself has already stopped bleeding. If you weren't already, you'd be dead because that bullet nicked an artery on the way in."

"Mary Jane, you must be more careful," Death mumbled, holding my hand in his. His face was filled with concern. He was a stalwart friend.

"I know," I said, eyes cast downwards.

"I shall summon my generals," the king said, eyeing the dilapidated cabin the bandits resided in with as much loathing as he eyed me. "We'll take this scum back to Hell. It's been years since we have had a public hanging."

"No," I cried, sitting upright. Pain coursed through my wing and shoulder.

"What," King Zagan snarled. "It's my duty, and yours, Nephilim!"

"Yes, it is, but I need more time," I stammered.

Death and Doc Holiday's eyebrows shot up. The question hung in the air between us: more time and for what?

"Mary Jane, what are you doing," Death finally whispered in my ear. "You can't stop the king from summoning his generals."

"You don't understand," I stammered. "There's video all over the internet. They're using the Hell horses' invincibility to crash through bank windows and clean out bank vaults. I have to find a way to explain it or make it look like a hoax. I don't think Uncle Lucifer would be pleased to see live proof Hell exists upside. I don't think we're supposed to do that, show ourselves the way we have been. It's like against Heaven and Hell's law or something."

"She's right, Zagan," Death agreed, facing down the demon king. Only Death would dare stand against him or not use his title.

King Zagan towered over my friend, a low rumble coming from deep inside the enraged demon's throat. His eyes burst into flames.

"Give Mary Jane some time to figure this out," Death said, standing his ground. "Let's say a week upside time. After that, you can personally retrieve the horse thieves and deliver them very publicly to Lucifer. Thanks to Mary Jane we know where they are hiding."

My heart sank.

One week? Impossible!

King Zagan grinned at my obvious distress.

How in Lucifer's name was I going to figure out a way to make the robberies look like a hoax and save both my dignity and Lucas' soul in the process?

"One week upside time it is," the king agreed. "I can't wait to see the look on Lucifer's face when I throw the horse thieves at his feet."

My mouth went dry.

"You three can get back on your own. I must set my guardsmen to work building the gallows," the king laughed. "The old ones fell down years ago."

I don't think I'd ever seen the demon king so happy. The thought chilled me to my core.

In a blink of an eye, King Zagan was gone. Life returned to what passed as normal. A light breeze rustled the leaves in the tree above my head. Crickets chirped. Frogs croaked. I hadn't realized they'd stopped until the familiar noises came back again.

"Come, I'll retrieve Mr. Jeepers and Binky and we'll take you to your mother's to recover," Death said, his voice brittle.

"All right," I replied, giving in.

"You have gotten yourself into a pickle," Doc Holiday said, letting out a long low breath.

"I'll figure something out," I said weakly. I had little choice.

Death started walking out into the meadow to go look for the two Hell horses when he stopped short.

The glint of moonlight on bone made me sit forward. The soft swish-swish of hooves walking through long grass overshadowed the caress of the wind in the meadow. Binky appeared before us. Lucas tipped his cowboy hat to Death as he rode by, unfazed.

A flame ignited in Death's blue eyes as his countenance darkened to match his mood. Whether the flame was because Lucas rode his horse or because of the state I was in remained to be seen.

"So that's the reason you haven't called your uncle yet," Doc Holiday chuckled. "You're in more than a pickle my dear you are a lobster locked inside a pot of boiling water."

I rolled my eyes at Holiday. He laughed heartily as he leaned against the tree watching the horse thief's every move.

"You're hurt," Lucas fumed. "I'll never forgive myself for this. I would have come quicker but I had to wait until everyone was asleep so I could sneak out. I should never have followed my brother into Hell."

"Then we'd never have met," I mumbled.

"She got too close to your fire and got burned, cowboy," Death hissed.

"Stop it, what's done is done," I griped, pushing myself painfully to my feet.

Lucas vaulted off of Binky's back only to realize too late that he could no longer see or hear me. He closed his eyes and leaned against Binky. When he opened them again, he could see me.

I smiled encouragement.

"Look, see, I'm fine," I lied. "I'll be good as new by tomorrow. It's one of the benefits of being an angel."

I held my hand up to stop Doc or Death from correcting me.

"Is it true," Lucas asked, looking Doc Holiday in the eye.

"True enough," Doc Holiday coughed.

"I'll take my mount back if you don't mind," Death said, hopping onto Binky's back. Binky turned his head away from Lucas and looked up at Death.

"You are a naughty boy," Death murmured, stroking a hand over Binky's neck bones.

"I hope I see you again," Lucas said, stepping away from Binky. "I know I keep repeating myself but I'm so sorry for all of this."

"Oh, you'll see her again, thief," Death chortled as he wheeled Binky around and rode off to retrieve Mr. Jeepers.

Tears fell unbidden from my eyes as Lucas turned and strolled silently back to the cabin, hands in his pockets, head hanging down.

"He didn't have to be so hard on him," I complained.

"Yes, he did, Mary Jane," Holiday corrected me.

I sulked. Doc was right, but I wasn't going to admit it.

"I'll go help Death retrieve Mr. Jeepers and then we'll ride to your mother's," he added.

I stood in the night, alone, watching the man I'd known for only a day walk away from me, his aura as wounded as my body. I held his fate in my hand. Lucas wasn't a bad man, but he wasn't a good man either. He robbed banks and stole horses. He stood by while his brother beat up Beetle, all because Beetle was in the way, but he was also sorry for his brother's deeds and his own inaction. I didn't want to watch King Zagan escort Lucas to Hell anymore than I wanted to see him or his friends hang.

And then there were the Hell horses. They stood by me, but left my care to follow a band of humans. There would be repercussions. Now wasn't the time to talk to Death or Doc Holiday about Binky's odd behavior either.

My heart broke in two.

I felt betrayed.

How strange to feel this way about a man I barely knew.

Doc Holiday returned leading Mr. Jeepers.

"You can only do what you can do, Mary Jane," he said sadly, cupping a hand for me to step into so that I could mount the Hell horse. There would be no stretching my wings and soaring the starry night for me for awhile.

I nodded absently, feeling the weight of the world and the afterlife upon my shoulders.

Death opened a rift to the in-between, the grey area between the realms of Heaven, Hell, Earth and Purgatory in which deities, angels, demons, and otherworldly creatures such as the Hell horses travelled from place to place in the blink of an eye. It was not the same as opening a portal directly into Heaven or Hell. It was slower, but it had to be used unless you were blindly going back to one of the realms.

I glanced wistfully over Doc Holiday's shoulder as he cradled me against his chest atop Mr. Jeepers. My right wing was wrapped in a metal splint; my left arm was in a sling. Blood once again coated my shirt and pants.

The moon was high in the sky. Its light cast long shadows across the meadow. Within these shadows a shape in the image of a man on a horse moved stealthily. I thought I heard Styx and Diablo trumpet a greeting as Mr. Jeepers leapt into the rift but the rift closed behind us so quickly I wasn't sure.

Darkness descended and I slumped forward, exhaustion overtaking me.

Mom and Apple Pie

I woke to the sound of arguing, my brain a foosball of fuzziness. My shoulder and wing didn't hurt, but my room was a blur.

I struggled to get out of bed, still dressed in the blood stained clothing I had worn the night before. The sun streamed through my bedroom window so it must be late morning already.

I tottered out of my bedroom and grabbed at the door sill to keep from falling. My wing splint caught the door's edge sending a wave of pain down my spine.

"Jupiter that hurts," I cried out.

"Stop it both of you, she's up," I heard my mother hiss. The argument in the kitchen stopped immediately and the house went quiet.

"Mom? Who's there," I mumbled disjointedly.

"Nobody," my mother said, rushing to my side. "The doc gave you some pretty strong painkillers last night. You must be hearing things."

"Oh, is he still here," I asked as she spun me back towards the bed.

"No, he and Death took the horses back to those dreadful horse thieves and then went back to Hell," my mother replied. "I haven't a clue why. Maybe you can explain it to me when you feel better. Doc had to go because Beetle still hasn't healed yet and Doc is worried about him. He'll be back later to check on you though. What an ugly affair this all is."

"It is," I nodded, my vision swimming as my mother helped me lay back down on the bed. That wasn't easy given my wing splint. "I'm sorry about the blood stains. And here I was thinking the competitive horse world was a tough place."

My mother didn't respond. That wasn't a good sign. Mom was never silent.

"Between dying and then returning home all beat up, you must be pretty angry with me," I half-sobbed. Crying always softened my mother up. Only half the tears were acting though.

"Right now, you need to rest," she smiled sadly, brushing my hair from my face like I was a five year-old. "I'll help you shower later and you can put on some fresh clothes. Your shoulder is still raw, but it's healing. Doc doesn't think you'll even have a scar."

"That's nice. The other one is pretty ugly," I sighed, meaning the hole in my back and chest where Diana's arrow pierced me. A seamstress in Hell Town stitched it up so that I didn't have an open wound anymore. Apparently, death wounds didn't heal. At least my boobs hid the stitches in the front. I asked her to do something funny and creative with the round hole in my back and she cross-stitched an outline of Casper the friendly ghost going boo in black and red. I thought it was cute.

"Close your eyes and sleep, sweetheart," she crooned.

"Okay," I murmured and then was fast asleep.

The next thing I knew the sun outside my window was rising and Doc Holiday was shaking me by the shoulder after what seemed like only minutes of peaceful dreams about me and Leyland winning the gold medal at the Olympics.

"Come on sleepy-head, wake-up."

"Go away, I'm stiff all over," I whined.

"Of course you are, you're dead," Death commented dryly. "And you need a shower. You smell like a wet dog after it's rolled in dung."

I opened one eye and glared up at the both of them.

"You've been asleep for twenty-four hours and time is ticking," Doc Holiday prodded me. "I'm going to take that splint off your wing now and you can start stretching it out."

"Fine," I grumbled, sitting up.

Even I could smell the scents of horse, stale sweat, sickness, and dried blood coming off me in waves. Shower it is, hot, very hot.

Doc gently removed the splint and I stood up.

71

"Ouch," I cried, stretching my wings so that the wing tips touched each wall. No, my wings hadn't grown, my bedroom was tiny. "That really hurts."

"It will for a couple more days," Holiday chuckled. "That's what happens when you get your feathers ruffled."

"They weren't ruffled, they were parted with real ammo," I grimaced. "When can I fly again?"

"Two days," he said, "but don't overdo it."

"Get cleaned up and come and eat," my mother called up the stairs. "You too, gentlemen, breakfast is almost done."

"Yes ma'am," Doc Holiday called back with a twirl of his moustache.

"We shall never decline a meal with a beautiful lady," Death laughed.

"Give me a break," I snorted.

I shouldered past them and into the hall, before slamming the bathroom door shut behind me in protest. Oh yes, I could be a petulant daughter when it came to the lineup of men wanting to date my mother.

Once I'd washed away the stink of defeat, I changed into some fresh clothes and went downstairs. Doc cut two slits into the back of my blouse for me to accommodate my wings. I was going to have to order yet another shirt from the seamstress in Hell Town. At the rate I was going through shirts, I was going to end up her best customer.

My mother laughed and batted her eyelashes at the two men. Doc beamed, his pale face taking on some actual color. Death flirted back. Cindy Lou Bligh, my mother, knew how to wrap a man around her finger; in this case, one immortal deity and one Western hero.

Holiday and Death sat down at the kitchen table. My mother deposited a heaping plate filled with scrambled eggs, homemade hash browns and bacon in front of them. They devoured the bacon in record time. I didn't have the heart to tell them it was veggie bacon.

"Thanks, mom," I said as she handed me a plate of the same. I was famished and finished my breakfast almost as quickly as the men sitting across from me.

"So," nodded Death, reaching for a toothpick, "we have five days left to figure out a way to make the world think Binky isn't real, the bank robberies were staged, and save that fellow you're sweet on."

"What fellow," my mother asked, a sly grin creeping across her face.

"Mary Jane has fallen hard for one of the bandits," Doc Holiday replied, his eyes alight with glee.

"Ooooh, spill the beans, child of mine," my mother kidded, taking a seat at the table.

"His name is Lucas," I sighed heavily. There was no point prolonging the pain. My mother would push me until I told her every little detail, which I didn't really want to do as I wasn't sure myself about my infatuation with the bandit. Was it love or had I simply lost my mind? That was the million dollar question.

"He's not like the rest of the gang, especially his brother, although they look alike," I said, pushing a fork around my empty plate.

"Binky seems to like him for some reason," Death grimaced."I don't see the appeal."

"Oh, you're just jealous," my mother chided Death.

Death harrumphed and crossed his arms in front of his chest.

"And acting like a child," I mumbled under my breath.

"He's quite a horseman," Doc Holiday added. "I'll give him that."

"He recognized me too," I nodded.

"I told you were famous," Mom said proudly. "Do you know how many of my clients watched you ride on the Sports Channel? A lot of them, especially after I told them your five hundred dollar rescue horse was out-jumping the hundred thousand dollar ones. You were the odds-on favorite to bring home a gold next year."

"Infamous now," I continued, my face reddening. "Lucas told me how he got into Hell and wound up stealing the horses. He and his brother and two friends were vacationing in Hawaii. They were at the top of Kilauea when Lucifer and I fell from Heaven and the angels attacked us. They saw King Zagan and his legions fight off the archangels. Lucas' brother stole a sword and chain mail from a fallen angel. It was his idea to sneak into Hell. Elijah took advantage of the gates being left open. The others followed along. I don't think any one of them thought about the consequences."

"Foolish mortals," Death snapped.

Mom put a hand over Death's to still his rage.

"Everyone is young and foolish in their youth, even you were I expect," Doc Holiday admonished the deity.

Death shrugged and let his anger fade.

"The only way I can think to make this work is to ask the seamstress in Hell to make us a horse costume that looks like Binky. It needs to be black with a complete horse skeleton on it. We can put it over Diablo and do a video showing a reveal... you know where we do the special effect and then yank off the costume to show the real horse underneath. We combine it with an interview with Lucas saying everything was faked. It was just a stunt. He can say that he and his friends were trying to break into acting."

"You think this Lucas will help you," Mom asked me.

"Yeah, I do," I blushed.

Would he? I hoped so.

"If he doesn't King Zagan will keep his word and haul him and his buddies back to Hell to face the music," Death rumbled.

I blushed once again, the heat scalding my face and neck, forever grateful to Death for not telling my mother what King Zagan had really said. I burped loudly, my stomach rebelling at the thought.

"Mary Jane!"

"Great breakfast, Mom," I said, forcing a smile.

My mind churned like a river boat wheel. How was I going to accomplish everything I had to do in five days? I mean, go to Hell and get a costume made for a Hell horse, convince Lucas to help me, shoot the video, and release it to the press? No pressure.

Mom pushed away from the table and opened the oven. I heard her fussing about as I picked at a fingernail. There was still some blood under my right index finger's nail.

"I made an apple pie for dessert," my mother smiled sweetly, returning with a freshly baked apple pie as if by magic. She slid the pie towards Doc Holiday.

"Dessert after breakfast," I guffawed.

"Why not," my mother shrugged.

I laughed aloud, forgetting my troubles as the smell of cinnamon, pastry and apple sugar made my mouth water.

Timing is Everything

Death, Doc Holiday and I sat at the table with a pen and paper outlining our plan.

"If you drop me off in Hell Town, I'll order the costume," Doc volunteered.

"I can do that," Death agreed. "Just make sure you put a rush on it."

"Great, so I just need to find someone to shoot the video because it needs to look professional," I said, nibbling on the end of my pen.

"I can do it," Mom chirped. "I'm good at it. I do all my own videos for my website and even have my own YouTube channel."

"Since when," I asked incredulously. Mom was a fitness fanatic not a camera geek.

"Since Abisai," she cooed. "You remember him, sweetheart. He was the photographer from Jamaica that did the boudoir photo of me hanging above my bed."

How could I forget? My mother was dressed as Lady Godiva, only she wasn't dressed at all save for one rickety palm frond, and her horse was a children's stuffed toy horse head on a pogo stick.

"He taught me basic photography and video editing before he went home," she beamed. "I have over three hundred thousand followers now. I live feed my morning work-outs so everyone in the world can follow along."

"I had no idea you were so talented," Doc Holiday said, his chin resting on his hand as he looked dreamy eyed at my mother.

"More than you can imagine," she whispered in his ear.

"Right, that's more than I want to know, let's get back to the plan," I barked.

"If we don't need to worry about finding a videographer," Death quipped, "why don't you come down to Hell Town with Doc and me? You'll heal faster there. We'll order the costume. You can ask Duke Zepar or Duke Berith if you can borrow Bucephalus or Wild Fire to ride upside to go talk to your boyfriend."

"Lucas is not my boyfriend," I hissed, painfully aware of how fragile my situation was at the moment.

Why was Death being such a pain?

"Looked that way to me," Doc said, his eyes still fixed upon my mother.

"Fine," I blurted out. That was my standard answer when I was being over-ruled or manipulated.

"Fine," Death quipped, crossing his arms.

I could tell he was enjoying tormenting me. His glacial blue eyes regarded me with a mixture of humor and defiance, a gaze I regularly saw in the mirror, when I was doing the same to him.

"What's got your knickers in a twist anyway," I demanded.

Two could play at this game.

Mother and Doc Holiday chuckled knowingly.

"I simply do not want to see you get your heart broken," Death sighed. "And mark my words, that bandit will break it."

"It's my heart to give away and mine to get broken," I murmured. We were friends after all, Death and I.

"That's the plan then," Doc said, shoving away from the table.

"Thank you for the wonderful meal," he added, planting a gentlemanly kiss on the back of my mother's hand.

"Anytime, Doc," she tittered.

"Yeah, time to go," I grumbled.

"Ditto," Death chuckled.

I shot Death a steely eyed look and he laughed heartily.

I gave my mother a hug and took hold of Death's hand. He clasped his fingers around mine and held on more tightly than he needed to as he portalled the three of us back to Hell. I bit my lip, praying that we wouldn't run into my Uncle Lucifer, but timing is everything.

The portal opened in front of the Hellfire Stables. Uncle Lucifer sat on an over turned feed bucket polishing his bridle as we arrived. Death dropped my hand immediately.

"Niece," Lucifer said without looking up from his work.

Yep, I was in trouble.

"Uncle," I replied, digging my boot toe into the edge of a cobble-stone.

"We'll get that errand done and see you in a bit," Death said, yanking Doc away by the arm.

"You have a report for me," Lucifer asked so softly I could barely hear him.

"I do, uncle," I nodded, squaring my shoulders. The left one tingled a bit, but all in all the pain was muffled compared to what it had been.

"I found the horse thieves, but there is a complication," I advised him.

"And what sort of complication warrants you're not calling me right away," my uncle rumbled, meeting my eyes. Lucifer's irises began to turn molten red. He was angry, but not rabid yet as the orbs hadn't gone pitch black. Red was a good thing.

"Well, first I discovered the bandits were using the horses to break into banks," I informed him, swallowing my fear. "The videos hadn't gone viral yet, most people believing they were fake, until recently when the internet exploded after a hiker posted a video of Binky in a park outside of Denver. I traced the location of that video and matched it up to some satellite maps and discovered their hideout. I confronted one of them and got shot in the process."

Okay, okay, I didn't actually confront Lucas, I kissed him, but my uncle didn't need to know that.

Silence ensued.

"Continue," Lucifer said, returning to cleaning his bridle, and his eyes returning to a mahogany brown.

Continue with what?

I blanched.

"And," I added, "I discovered how they got into Hell, where they got the angel's sword from, and have formed a plan to bring the Hell horses back home with the help of Death and Doc Holiday. I also have an idea on how to stem the damage done by the Binky and bank robbery videos circulating upside."

"A good day's work then," he nodded approval, "and what of the horse thieves? What are your plans to bring them to justice?"

Oooh, I didn't like the sound of that last part. What lies had King Zagan told my uncle or bragged about to Lucifer's informants at the pub?

Well, I could be devious too.

"King Zagan showed up unannounced and wants to personally escort them back to Hell and hang them publicly in the middle of the town square," I said. "The king is overstepping his bounds and I told him so. It's for you to decide what happens to them."

Lucifer put down the bridle and stood up. He sauntered over to me and wrapped me in a warm embrace.

"Ouch," I gasped. "Watch my wing uncle, it still hurts."

"They'll pay dearly for hurting you," my uncle assured me. "Nobody harms my favorite niece."

"Thank you, uncle," I stammered, feeling bad for holding back the whole truth, especially the part where I confess to falling head-over-wings for one of the bandits.

"So, how are you getting back upside if you can't fly," the devil inquired.

"I thought I'd ask Duke Berith or Duke Zepar if I can borrow one of their horses," I replied, my confidence returning. "Doc says it will be another day or two before my wing fully heals."

"Nonsense, take Brimstone," Lucifer offered. "When it's time to bring the boys back home, they won't dare defy him."

"Okay, but he won't hurt the horses for their defiance of you, right," I cried, pleading the horses' case. "They were just bored. They wanted to go on an adventure like in the old days. You can't blame them for that."

"I suppose not," Lucifer agreed, scratching his chin with a dirty finger. His hands were rough and covered with saddle oil and liniment. "I shall have a chat with Brimstone before you go. I love the boys, you know that, but they did disobey me. I can't appear weak down here, Mary Jane. There is trouble brewing and I need to put up a strong front."

"That's all I ask, uncle," I begged him. "Give them the benefit of the doubt. Perhaps there is a 'Grand Plan' at play that none of us realize."

"A 'Grand Plan'," Lucifer guffawed using air quotes to tease me. "The only Grand Plan in Hell is mine. Keep Father out of it."

"Yes, sir," I replied, contrite.

"Now, fill me in on these exploits of yours while we go and re-trieve Brimstone from the outer pasture, I want to hear all about how these bandits came up with the idea to steal my horses," my uncle grinned, wrapping an arm around my waist like he used to do when I was a child.

Once again a shadow crossed my peripheral vision. I glanced sideways rather than turn my head, and glimpsed Chappie leaning against the shaded side of the barn, watching us, and listening to every word. Trouble was definitely afoot; I could feel it in my bones.

I was so unnerved by Chappie I didn't realize I had launched into a recount of Lucas' story, not even remotely thinking about how to explain how I knew all of these details.

All's Fair in Love & War

"Brimstone, take care of Mary Jane," my uncle whispered in the black stallion's ear. "Bring her back safe and sound."

"Thank you, uncle," I said, a lump forming in my chest. With everything Lucifer had on his plate, he still took the time to care for me. Make no mistake, my uncle was vain, powerful, womanizing, and sometimes brutal, but he had always been loving and supportive of me, looking at me more as a daughter than a niece.

"I will see you upside in a few days," Lucifer said, stepping aside to let Brimstone and me through the gates of Hell. Geryon saluted me as I rode through the gates as if I was a soldier heading to war.

I rode along the pathway bordering the River Styx for awhile, past the landing where hundreds of souls, if not a thousand or more, were being processed by other damned souls. Some of the lost looked befuddled, others embarrassed, but most were explosive and angry. A platoon of cruel faced demons snapped short stubby whips, driving the lost soul's forward en masse towards the check point. I sympathized with the souls, but they were all here for a reason. It was not my place to judge. Because of my genes and not my actions, I was damned.

The River Styx flowed quickly here. Not but two hundred yards from the processing area was a four hundred foot waterfall with sharp boulders protruding from the base. Steep cliffs over a half mile high rose above the river. The sky above was a mix of cloudy mist and smoke. The air was humid. The only sounds were that of weeping souls, the cracking of whips, and the kettle drum thrum of the falls ahead.

If any soul thought to outrun their lot and dove into the water to escape, their soul would shatter on the enchanted rocks below the falls and they would wind up either back in line where they had first started or they would cease to exist. Uncle Lucifer never told me the how or the why of which soul made it and which one didn't. I had a feeling it was chance.

"Come on, Brimstone, let's get out of here, it's too depressing," I murmured, squeezing the stallion into a lope. "Open the portal and read my thoughts. There is a fast running creek at the base of the meadow below the cabin where the herd is."

The stallion snorted in understanding and broke into a gallop. I tucked my wings against my back and grinned, the wind whipping my lollipop colored hair out behind me as I let the stallion run free. The sound of the falls grew to deafening proportions as Brimstone leapt into the mist.

Within the blink of an eye, the stallion was bucking out our arrival.

Neither the creek, nor the mountain river the creek joined east of there, were as mighty as the River Styx, but it was stunning all the same. Birds, butterflies and dragonflies flitted over the babbling brook. The shadow of an eagle swept across the creek bed. We galloped along the grassy banks to the bottom end of the meadow staying close to the water so we wouldn't be seen.

"Brilliant, Brimstone, perfect landing," I praised the horse, running a hand beneath the stallion's majestic mane.

Brimstone frolicked beneath me.

My grin widened to epic proportions.

I didn't know what time it was, but I suspected it was getting close to five o'clock in the afternoon. The sun was getting low on the horizon and a cool breeze lightened the summer heat.

I reined up on the rise overlooking the pasture where the Hell horses had been grazing the day before yesterday. The horses were there. Lucas and the man called Caleb sat on the porch playing cards. They appeared to be arguing good-naturedly as Lucas threw his cards down on the table and raised his hands in surrender. Caleb gleefully swept the pile of bills off the table and into his pocket.

I sat there for awhile watching the two friends interact. Brimstone relaxed underneath me. We were downwind of the Hell horses so none of them had noticed us yet. My mind raced. I was here now, but how was I going to get Lucas alone? How too would I stop the Hell horses from racing to us once they saw or scented the stallion?

"I think we better back off, Brimstone," I sighed. "Let's keep things quiet until I get a chance to meet Lucas alone."

The stallion flicked an ear back towards me as I signaled him to head into the trees. I knew he was annoyed. He was ready for action.

"There will be a time and place for that," I whispered, leaning across his neck and hugging him.

The stallion licked his lips in supplication and we wandered into the tree line. We circled around until we located a patch of lush green grass growing amidst the tall poplars. I dismounted and took off the stallion's bridle. He wouldn't leave me. He was under orders to guard me.

"Munch away my friend, I'm going to go climb that old fir over there and see if I can see the cabin," I informed the horse, pointing to an ancient fir on the edge of the meadow within the stallion's sightline. Its lower limbs sagged, many were broken off. It would be an easy climb since flying was still out of the question.

The stallion shot me a penetrating look as if to say, 'fine by me, but don't go farther than that', as if the horse were my boss. I chuckled aloud at the idea.

I ducked under the boughs of the fir and started to climb. It was scratchy going. Red welts covered my arms by the time I got as far up as I could go without breaking the top off the tree. I had already learned the hard way that I was as good as human when it came to Mother Nature's bounty.

The sun started to drop below the hills. Blue sky turned yellow and then red. Lucas and his friend went into the house as smoke began rising from the cabin's chimney. I could imagine him inside with his brother and friends putting a cook pot on the stove and readying themselves for dinner.

I wasn't prepared for the four gun toting cowboy hat wearing bandits slamming their way out of the house, leather slickers billowing out behind them as they went to round up the Hell horses. I noticed Elijah had a sword hilt poking out of a scabbard on the same side as his gun belt. It didn't take a genius to know it was the fallen angel's sword.

"Hell's bells," I swore, chafing the inside of my legs raw as I scuttled down the tree.

"Brimstone, come," I yelled, racing to the patch of grass the stallion had all but obliterated.

Brimstone trotted the last few paces to me, his stride long and powerful. I slipped the bridle from my shoulder and over his head.

"I don't know how we're going to do it, but we have to follow the men without being seen," I told the stallion as I leapt aboard him. "We need to be quiet and try not to let your brothers scent or hear us too. Think we can do that?"

The stallion turned his head and gave me a look that said volumes about my lack of IQ in his opinion. I was glad my uncle and my mother weren't there to see it.

Brimstone then did something I didn't know was possible. His coat started to shimmer like water trickling over a rock. The shimmer started at his legs and worked its way up his chest, head and neck, and then legs and torso, until we were but a mirage of wind in the grass.

The bandits saddled their horses and rode out, jogging up a grassy knoll to the narrow deer trail that led down to the creek and then up the rocky slopes to the lookout where the old fire tower was.

Brimstone and I followed at a discreet distance. While I could not see them, neither could they see me. Neither they nor the Hell horses even once turned to see who followed.

I daren't even whisper to the stallion. His abilities amazed me. I wished I could tell him so, but stealth was paramount.

Suddenly, the group halted in the open ground that surrounded the fire tower where the overgrown road leading to it once was. Brimstone and I followed suit, stopping on the edge of the clearing to watch them.

Elijah raised the sword and slashed downwards with it, opening a rift to the in-between. A waft of thick swirling fog rolled out of the teardrop shaped tear in time and space. He cantered Styx into it, the others galloping in after him.

"Can you follow them, Brim," I asked the stallion, urging him into a gallop. "Will our glimmer hold in the in-between?"

The stallion grunted and squealed a high pitched command. His eyes blazed. Dragon fire spewed out of his nostrils and his soft coat took on a hellish glean, the hairs turning to blue black scales before my eyes. The air in front of us rippled. Reality split in two as a rift opened in front of us with a sickening ripping sound. Brimstone coughed up firefly-like sparks which caused the fog racing towards us to recoil as if it were a living entity. The horse's hooves turned into claws. His tail coiled into a long barbed weapon as massive bat like wings sprouted from his shoulders. I had to lift my legs and hang on for dear life as the wings formed and unfurled.

No wonder the Hell horses obeyed Brimstone's every command. He wasn't just a horse, but a shape shifting dragon.

"Find them, Brimstone," I yelled, my voice muffled in the vacuum of the in-between. Sheets of mist and curling wraiths parted before us, dragon fire lighting our way and illuminating the path the bandits had taken. The Hell horses hoof prints glowed in the swirling layers of gray.

We followed the four horsemen's tracks until they abruptly ended at what looked like a ragged seam in a tapestry.

Brimstone shot a fire bolt out of his mouth.

The wall between worlds blasted open.

I gasped as we flew through the opening and soared into the air above what I thought was Arizona. Desert plains swept from horizon to horizon. Hundreds of cacti dotted the striated landscape. A sea of brilliant reds, pinks and yellows shimmered off of Brimstone's wings and scales as we glided high in the sky. My eyes wept at the beauty and thrill of it all. I reveled at the wind in my face and fervently wished I could stretch out my wings and fly beside the dragon whose back I straddled as the sun went down.

Far below I spotted the four bandits galloping across the desert as dusk descended. Lights popped on in the city in the distance. A halo of white surrounded the city, heralding mans presence.

"There they are, my friend," I cheered. "We'll stay hidden, Brimstone, until we know which bank they're going to rob in that city up ahead. I'm thinking they're going to wait until late and hit it after hours. We'll watch for the moment when we can catch Lucas on Binky by himself. When we do, I need you to command the Hell horses to ignore us. It isn't time for them to come home yet. We've other plans to set in place first."

Brimstone turned his head and fixed his fiery dragon eyes upon me. He nodded once and then switched his attention back to the *Ghost Rider Gang*.

Flying through the skies on a dragon was more exhilarating than I ever could have imagined. I didn't want the journey to end, but night fell quickly in the desert and the band of robbers stopped to build a fire beneath a sandstone abutment. There was a spring nearby. I saw Caleb lead the horses to it, all except for Binky who stayed at Lucas' side.

Binky sure had it bad for Lucas. I understood the Hell horse completely. It seemed I was in the same boat. All I could think about was the taste of his lips on mine and the color of his bedroom eyes.

I was doomed.

Brimstone circled down to ground level and abruptly changed back into the thickly muscled corded stallion as his hooves hit the ground. He arched his neck and pawed the earth, the magic glimmer returning to shield us both from prying eyes.

We walked over to the spring and waited for our moment.

Caleb leaned against the rock formation as the horses drank from the spring one at a time. I could see his freckled face clearly. It was so innocent. Caleb didn't look like any bank robbers I'd ever met, and believe me, there were loads of them in Hell Town.

Brimstone inhaled and let out a shrill whinny.

Darn the Hell horse, so much for my being in command.

Styx flew backwards at the sound almost tearing Caleb's arm

out of the socket.

"You blew our cover, Brim," I croaked, running a calming hand down his neck. His flesh was hot to the touch.

"Whoa boy," Caleb shouted, barely able to hold onto the mustang.

The Hell horses snorted, turning as one to look in our direction.

I felt, rather than saw, Brimstone bunch his muscles as he lifted his front end high off the ground, tucking his neck in, and snapping at his rebellious brethren. I almost fell off such was his powerful lunge towards them. My hands grabbed a fistful of mane and my legs hugged his torso. At Lucifer's suggestion, I rode bareback with just a bitless bridle in the stallion's mouth for ease of maneuvering. I was regretting that decision.

"What's got into them," Lucas yelled, racing to the spring to help, Binky trotting obediently behind him. The bone horse skidded to a stop beside the others. His head lifted as he looked in our direction, but he suddenly dropped it and turned away.

The other horses settled quickly and dropped their heads in supplication. Obviously, the glimmer we hid behind didn't mask Brimstone's smell or his call, but what was important was the horses had obeyed his order without question.

"Must have been a coyote or something," Cable replied, relaxing.

"You think a coyote would scare any of these guys," Elijah said, appearing out of the dark. Ronin stalked out of the shadows behind him, his Colt raised, ready for action.

"Who knows what gets under the skin of these stallions," Caleb shrugged. "They didn't come with a manual. I don't think Chicken Soup for the Hell Horses' Soul has been written yet."

"Don't get any ideas either," Lucas chuckled.

The tension in the group eased and Ronin holstered his gun.

"We'll leave in twenty. Come and eat, Caleb, we've saved some bush beans for you," Elijah laughed.

"I'll watch over the horses while you eat, Caleb," Lucas said, taking the reins from his friend's hands.

"Wahoo, beans," Caleb chortled. "We can back the horses up to the vault and all let loose at once. No vault in the world could stand up to our farts."

"Neither would we," Lucas roared.

I smiled. If they really wanted to explode a steel door inwards they should give the beans to the horses.

As soon as the three men disappeared from whence they came, I walked the stallion into the open, allowing him to drop the glimmer we hid behind. This was my chance.

The horses started, their ears pricking forward, steam billowing from their nostrils. Styx arched his neck and puffed out his chest, yanking Lucas off his feet and into him. Lucas inhaled sharply, the contact with the buckskin mustang's flesh allowing him to see us.

My face broke into a lopsided grin and I waved sheepishly.

"Mary Jane," he whispered hoarsely, racing towards me, and then wind-milled to a stop. Both of us realized at the same time that when he lost contact with Styx, he lost sight of me.

Brimstone pinned back his ears and snapped his teeth.

"Stop it, Brim, he's alright," I mumbled to the horse, slipping off the stallion's back.

As one, the Hell horses bowed a leg to Brimstone like he was their king. Styx, whose mustang blood wanted him to fight for dominance, was the last to bend a knee, but Brimstone was far more than just a horse and Styx knew it.

"You're alive," Lucas gasped, reaching blindly for me. "And healed up? How did you do it so quickly? Oh, right, you're an angel."

"Binky," Lucas called into the night.

Binky responded instantly. The handsome bandit placed a hand on the skeletal horse's neck and then leaned against his rib cage.

I raced to Lucas' side. He wrapped his arms around my waist while still keeping his back against the bone horse's rib cage lest Lucas lose me. My heart soared as I felt the steady beat of his heart against me. I knew deep inside he loved me as much as I loved him.

There, it was out there! I loved him fool that I was. I'd laughed at my girlfriends when this happened to them and here I was throwing caution to the wind.

"We don't have long," I gushed. "Lucifer knows where you are, but that's not the biggest problem."

Lucas scowled. His back went rigid. His arms fell to his sides and he pulled away while still maintaining some contact, though now feather light.

"Look, King Zagan has vowed to bring you all back to Hell in three days and hang you in the city square. It's a power play and you, your brother, and your friends are caught in the middle of it," I said forcefully. "You've broken umpteen laws by getting caught on video robbing banks using the Hell horses, not to mention the videos people took of you riding Binky through the woods. If Heaven gets involved, it will mean war, and I mean a real fire and brimstone demons versus angels Armageddon with Earth in the middle kind of war. Thousands if not millions will die."

"I see," Lucas replied stiffly.

"Lucas, I'm trying to save you," I said, my resolve crumbling.

Was I that stupid, that desperate to find love, I was willing to sacrifice everything for a man who maybe loved me?

"Why," he asked solemnly.

"Because I love you," I whimpered, angry at myself for being such a chump, "and I love my mom, and my horse, and my girlfriends. I don't want to see you or anyone else die."

A smile creased his lips and he picked me up off the ground and swung me in a circle before planting his lips on mine and kissing me with a deep longing that I understood and responded with in kind.

I burst into tears.

Okay, maybe I wasn't a chump.

"What can I do to help stop this war," he murmured in my ear.

"Doc Holiday and Death are getting a costume made for Diablo," I replied breathlessly, feeling the heat of his body against mine. "It will make him look like Binky."

"That was Doc Holiday and Death who helped you," Lucas started, shocked.

"Yeah, Doc's a fan of yours, Death agrees with my uncle," I quipped. "Anyway, I need you to go on record as saying the robberies and Binky were all a hoax so you and the boys could break into Hollywood."

Lucas gaped at me. He clicked his mouth shut when he realized I wasn't joking.

"Okay," he snorted. "If you think it will work, I'll do it. It's not every day I get to save the Universe."

"Good," I grinned, wiping away my tears.

When had I turned into such a sap?

"I'll pick you up at sunrise tomorrow morning."

"And who is going to film this video," he asked, his cheeks still flushed.

"My mother," I shrugged sheepishly. "She learned how from a Nigerian photographer she dated a few years ago."

"I can't wait to meet her," he chuckled.

Brimstone nudged me in the back.

"I guess you have to go," Lucas nodded glancing sideways at Lucifer's prized stallion. "Just so you know, I told my brother this is the last bank job I'm doing. Someone's bound to get hurt. I never wanted to do it in the first place. It's high time I stood up to him. Caleb agreed with me. We're both done."

I kissed my love one more time and he kissed me back, hard.

"Lucas, it's time," his brother shouted.

"See you tomorrow," I moaned, breaking away from him.

I vaulted onto Brimstone and wheeled around. Brimstone placed the glimmer back over us and we galloped across the desert. I swear I could feel Lucas' eyes fixed on my back.

"Okay, Brim, let's head back to Hell, pick up the Binky costume, and then head to my mom's," I told the stallion, a stupid grin on my face. I could still feel the impression of Lucas' lips on mine.

"I don't usually pray to you, since you hate me and all, but God, I could really use your help with this," I said, glancing up at the stars.

God didn't answer, but that wasn't a big surprise. My prayers had gone unanswered all my life.

Before I could say 'Peter Pan', I was cantering Brimstone down Main Street in Hell Town, the looks of envy, and some rage, on several demons' faces not going unnoticed by me or my mount.

Murphy's Law

I was almost at the seamstress's shop which was kitty corner to the Satyr Pub when Doc Holiday burst through the door, a bulky parcel tied up with string tucked under Holiday's arm. Death strode quickly out of the pub at the same time, the two almost colliding.

"Where is she now," Doc Holiday asked Death righting himself.

"I've no idea, but I have to go upside, duty calls," Death grumbled. "Right in the middle of my second pint too."

"I'm here," I laughed, trotting Brimstone towards the two. "Is that the Binky costume?"

"It is," Holiday grinned, holding up the parcel. "Wait until you see it, the seamstress outdid herself. Did you know you're her favorite customer?"

"You're riding Brimstone?" Death huffed, interrupting.

"Yes and yes, to both your questions," I laughed.

Brimstone shook out his mane and eyed Death dubiously. Only a Hell horse could wrinkle his nose and look down upon someone so effectively.

"Everything is set," I grinned. "Lucas agreed to help us shoot the video. I'm meeting with him at sunrise tomorrow."

"You're meeting him faster than that," Death said. "Your gang of bank robbers just shot a security guard. Lucas stepped in. You need to come with me – now!"

"Nooo, I just left him," I wailed, my heart breaking. "You're serious?"

"I am," Death sighed. "That Ronin is a hard case. There's no time to fill you in."

"Go with Death, I'll take Brimstone back to the stables," Doc said gently, his eyes meeting Death's. "That or stay with me if you can't face it."

My whole body went rigid.

"What do you mean 'Lucas stepped in'," I spat, my eyes narrowing as I looked Death square in the eye.

"In or out," was all my friend replied.

My jaw set, determination dried my tears.

"I'm going."

"There's a hell of a shootout going on upside," Death warned me. "Stay close, Mary Jane."

"You know what, I'm going with you," Holiday jumped in, tossing the costume into the hands of a drunken demon exiting the pub.

"Take that and Lucifer's horse to the stables," the doc ordered the confused demon.

"Brimstone can make his own way back to the stable," I said, knotting the reins over the stallion's neck. "Go find Lucifer and tell him what's happening."

Brimstone instantly sprang into a gallop, demons and Hell's denizens jumping out of his way as he made a beeline for the devil's mansion.

Death nodded. Doc and I placed a hand on each of his shoulders and we were back upside in the blink of an eye.

It was pandemonium. Bullets whizzed by our faces. Red, white and blue lights flashed. Swat teams were lined up outside the bank. There were police snipers on the roofs across the road from the bank; sniper rifles pointing into the bank's smashed windows. Alarms rang.

"This is just like old times," Doc Holiday grinned, tugging a cigar from his waist pocket and lighting it.

"Come on," Death smirked, walking through the rain of bullets. "Stand behind me, Mary Jane. Doc can't get shot, he's a ghost up here, but you can."

I nodded and kept a hand on Death's shoulder as we crunched our way through the shards of glass littering the street and then climbed through the bank's broken window.

The Grim Reaper nodded to us from behind the cashier's counter. Mr. Jeepers stood behind him, the horse all business now that his rider was here. Ronin and Elijah's six guns were smoking as they stood on either side of the open window firing at the swat team. Both Styx and Diablo were nowhere to be seen, but Binky also stood on the far side of the cashier's counter, his head bent in sorrow.

"Lucas," I screamed, vaulting over the counter.

Caleb cradled Lucas' head in his lap, tears streaming down the young cowboy's face. Lucas had two bloody holes in his side and one in his arm. The security guard on the floor beside Lucas had one bullet hole in the center of his chest. The guard's gun lay on the floor beside him.

The guard gurgled, blood dripping from his mouth.

I raced to Lucas' side.

"Mary Jane," Lucas stuttered weakly. Now at death's door, he could see me without the help of a Hell horse. "Guess I blew your plan."

"What plan, bro," Caleb sobbed.

I knelt beside Caleb and reached out to cup Lucas' face in my hands. Tears flowed freely as Caleb and I cried the tears Binky couldn't.

Death motioned the Grim Reaper to take the guard's precious soul to Heaven.

Lucas heard the guard's final death rattle and glanced over at him, his eyes rounding as he saw the Grim Reaper retrieve the man's soul. Mr. Jeepers accompanied the Grim Reaper and the guard's soul on their journey to the Pearly Gates where the soul would be judged by Saint Peter, my arch nemesis. The guard was a good man. Saint Peter would welcome him, I thought bitterly.

It wasn't my finest hour.

"I'm sorry," Lucas wept.

"Don't be sorry, brother," Caleb moaned, wiping his tears away. "Oh, wait; you're not talking to me are you? The angel's here, isn't she?"

Caleb looked me in the eye, but hadn't the power to see me.

Still, he seemed to know where I was. Perhaps witch blood flowed through his veins.

"Caleb, get over here," Ronin hissed from his place by the window.

"No! I'm done," Caleb snarled. "What's the matter with you? A man is dead and Lucas is dying. Good Lord, Elijah, what about you? This is your brother laying here."

"I can't get there without getting shot too," Elijah bellowed.

Doc Holiday placed a comforting hand on my shoulder as Lucas closed his eyes.

"Can't you do something," I begged Death.

My friend shook his head.

I wailed in earnest. The Grim Reaper was back. Mr. Jeepers hadn't returned with him.

"It's his time, Mary Jane," Death said. He waved the Grim Reaper forward.

"No, stop," I pleaded, a waterfall of tears flowing down my face, "or at least let me go with you to take his soul to Hell. Maybe Uncle Lucifer will show him some mercy?"

"He's not going to Hell, Mary Jane," the reaper whispered sadly.

"He gave his life to try and save another man's life," Death murmured. "He has been forgiven."

"Is this your idea of a joke," I yelled, shaking my fist in my friend's face.

"No," Death sighed. "I would never do this to you."

I bet it was God's doing.

"Let's just heap more pain on the Nephilim? Are you wondering how much it will take to break me? Congratulations. Well done," I screamed, turning my attention to Heaven.

My heart shattered as the reaper reaped Lucas' soul and the love of my life was gone. I gasped the pain in my chest even worse than when the arrow pierced it.

I heard a series of disjointed screams as I cried over the empty shell that had once belonged to the man I loved. I had never believed in love at first sight until it happened to me. In fact, I had avoided it all my life. Who could love an ugly half-breed like me?

That was what I told myself over and over again until I believed it.

"Where are the horses," I stuttered as the gunfire outside increased. I stood and wiped my face with my sleeve. My whole body shook with grief, but I had a job to do. I could tend to the horses and call my uncle now that Lucas' soul was safe from damnation.

"I guess their escapade soured when a life was taken," Doc Holiday replied.

"Two lives," I sniffled.

"They've gone home I expect," Death muttered.

"What are those," Caleb squealed, racing to join Ronin and Elijah by the window.

Mary Jane turned towards the window. The gunfire had stopped. A deathly silence ensued followed by a screech of claws on asphalt and the sound of beating wings.

"Demons," Elijah spat, drawing the angel sword from the scabbard on his hip.

How I ever thought Elijah looked like Lucas was beyond me. The angry man standing at the window, glowing sword in one hand, Colt in the other, looked nothing like his gentle natured brother. The two had nothing in common but blond hair.

"Looks like it's going to be a busy night," Death sighed.

Doc Holiday and I joined Death at the window. King Zagan and a squad of flying demons descended upon the scene. The king of demons and his men waded past the bullet ridden police cars and vans, not giving the officers hiding behind them a second thought, until the swat teams opened fire. Bullets bounced off the demon's leathery hides. The snipers on the roof tops fired at the demon horde, but it had no effect.

"Come out, come out wherever you are," the king laughed maniacally as he strode confidently towards the bank. Two generals and a dozen personal guards flanked him while the rest of the squadron kept the police at bay.

"What on upside are you doing here, Zagan," Death snarled. "You've broken at least a dozen hierarchal laws. Isn't the damage these mortals have already done bad enough?"

"I'm the King of Demons," Zagan barked. "I can do whatever I want. Who is going to stop me?"

"Oh, there are at least a dozen deities I can think of who would be delighted to do that," Holiday chuckled. "And they're a whole lot mightier than you."

"I'm here for the horse thieves," the king growled, ignoring Doc Holiday.

"It's not their time," Death smirked, folding his arms across his chest in defiance.

"Stand aside and I'll solve that problem right now," King Zagan laughed cruelly.

Elijah charged. He swung his sword at the king's head. The king dodged it. A superior grin spread across the king's face as his generals swooped in and easily disarmed Elijah. Death stepped in to stop it, but a dozen of the king's guardsmen restrained him.

"Binky, no," Death yelled as the bone horse raced in to help his master.

Doc Holiday grabbed me by the arm and hauled me out of the way.

"LUCIFER," I screamed, the building rattling in response.

"It's too late, Mary Jane," Doc Holiday croaked as he threw me to the ground to avoid the hail of bullets that pounded the bank walls behind us.

"Yes, he can," I grimaced, pointing down the street to where the devil had appeared out of nowhere.

Lucifer's Colts jumped in his hands as his silver capped bullets tore through Zagan's regiment. The demons wailed as they fell under the Prince of Darkness' onslaught.

Lucifer's leather duster flew out behind him as the black stallion leapt into the fray. Both Brimstone and Lucifer's eyes were alight with hellfire. The devil was in his element and reveling in it. The black clad man on the black stallion with guns blazing unleashed a fury that the world hadn't seen in two thousand years.

"Now that's how you make an entrance," Doc Holiday murmured in admiration.

"You're too late and too slow, Lucifer," the king snarled as he and his generals restrained the bandits and opened a portal. "Hell is mine. Everything has been set in motion."

What did King Zagan mean by that?

What was set in motion?

Poor Caleb looked in shock, his bound hands trembling, his face ashen, and his eyes downcast and unseeing. Elijah looked like a caged animal, eyes wild, and face feverish. Ronin was purple faced and angry with a dirty rag stuffed in his mouth. I had little sympathy for the last two.

"You're done, Zagan," Lucifer spat, turning his guns on the king.

"No, you are," the king chortled, stepping through the portal with the three bandits and two of his generals.

"Attack," Zagan screamed at his soldiers before disappearing back to Hell.

"Get my niece out of here," Lucifer yelled at Doc Holiday.

"Take Binky," Death ordered Holiday over the din of the fighting as the demons converged upon my uncle.

Gun smoke filled the air. Demons snarled. Men screamed.

All of a sudden a portal opened in the sky and my father, the archangel Gabriel, barreled out of it, his fourteen foot wide wings tucked behind him, golden sword drawn. Behind him swooped the archangels Michael and Raphael.

My mouth fell open.

Three archangels coming to the aid of the devil was unheard of?

Surely, the world was ending.

I barely recognized my father, it had been so long since I'd seen him, but it was definitely Gabriel. My mother had but one picture of my father holding me as a baby. He looked the same as in the picture, walnut colored hair and wings, bronzed skin, an angelic aura surrounding him.

Doc Holiday lifted me into Lucas' saddle which was still on Binky's back, and then swung up behind me. He shortened the reins and held Binky tightly coiled, ready to spring.

"Are you coming with us," Doc shouted at Death.

"No," Death snarled, his face a mask of hatred for the demons who dared rebel against Lucifer. "Go!"

Holiday nodded and dug his heels into Binky's ribs.

Swords clashed against swords. Fire and lightning collided. The police officers, snipers, and swat teams ran for their lives as demon and archangel clashed.

Binky opened a portal and we galloped through it.

Fire and Brimstone

We arrived at the Hellfire Stables to find it in a shambles. Beetle, head still bandaged, rushed from horse to horse, duke to duke, making sure tack was secure despite his head injury. There was fresh blood staining the white bandage red.

Duke Berith, Duke Alocer, and Duke Zepar were already on their horses, the horses in full armor. Bucephalus danced beneath Duke Zepar, his silver and brass armored breast plate and croupiere on his flanks clinking like a silverware wind catcher. His neck criniere of armored pieces shone like the grille of an antique car. Duke Berith on Hell Fire was also fully armored, the candy apple red horse's nostrils flared, the red armor it wore a match to the bold red knight aboard him. I didn't know Duke Alocer; the lion faced knight, well. He was fearsome to look at, the only knight not wearing a helmet, his teeth bared, and his golden lion's mane shining beneath the stable lighting. He looked ready to rip anyone who crossed him limb from limb which I suspect he was.

"It appears we arrived just in time," Doc Holiday joked.

I didn't see the humor in it. The love of my life had gone to Heaven. I'd never see Lucas again. I never had a chance to tell him I wasn't a heavenly angel, but a despised half-breed so he had no idea that he'd never see me again either. What a mess I'd made of everything.

"Mary Jane," Beetle cheered, racing over to take Binky's reins. "You're okay."

"For the moment," I said as Doc Holiday and I dismounted.

"Holiday," Duke Zepar shouted at the former lawman. "Mount up. Take Styx or Diablo. It's time those two Hell horses remembered who they are and what side they are on."

"I'll take Styx," the doc said. "Saddle him up for me Beetle while I retrieve my guns. I know I have some silver bullets somewhere too, but they're all in my cottage."

Beetle gave me a quick hug and raced off to put Binky in his stall and saddle Styx. Styx and Diablo kicked impatiently at their stall doors.

"What's happening," I trembled. I could ride anything with four legs, but I wasn't a soldier.

"Asroth, fetch a breast plate, a mail shirt, and a short sword from the armory for Mary Jane," Duke Zepar called to his footman. The young demon raced off to fulfill the duke's command. He couldn't have been any older than Beetle.

"But I don't know how to fight," I panted, my terror mounting. This was too much to expect of me. Yes, I was fearless on a horse, but war was another matter. I doubted I could kill anyone even to save myself.

"You need protection," the duke explained. "King Zagan and three of the other dukes are staging a coup. The huntress has joined them. Lucifer is still upside. We have to defend the city. Zagan and the huntress will be targeting you."

My blood ran cold. I was a target… again! The goddess Diana had betrayed Lucifer. Was it truly her that killed me or was it King Zagan or possibly one of his generals? Had they shot me in order to start the war rolling? The thought chilled me. Was I really and truly a pawn in all of this?

"Then I better stay with you, sir," I replied, shivers rippling up and down my spine while goose bumps partied up a storm on my arms. "I'll ride Charlemagne. He's wider and taller than the rest and trained in war maneuvers. Sorry, Diablo."

Diablo snapped at me over his stall door.

"Stop that you stupid beast," the duke commanded the Hell horse. "I've a general who needs a mount. You'll be in the thick of it."

The stallion pricked his ears forward but continued to pound his leg against the stall door when a fiery cannon ball struck the yard. Cobble stones exploded outwards, peppering the stone walls of the stable. Diablo squealed as the top of his stall's outer wall shattered, showering him with fist sized rocks.

Doc Holiday dodged the rearing horses in the aisles as he ran to Styx. Beetle hauled the saddled buckskin mustang out of his stall and then grabbed Diablo for the demon general that was also dodging eager warhorses. Holiday vaulted onto Styx's back and trotted away, head down, to join the dukes who were already galloping out of the stable yard without me.

I didn't know what to do so I just stood there feeling like a fool.

The duke's aide raced in carrying chainmail, a breast plate, a helmet, and a sword. He quickly yanked the chainmail over my head and breasts, raising his golden eyes to me, a smirk on his face as he squished my boobs beneath it. He fastened the leather ties at the side while Beetle saddled and armored Charlemagne, the massive warhorse chomping at the bit to join the battle. Zepar's general snatched the lead rope out of Beetle's hand, leapt onto Diablo's back and trotted out of the stable as is – no bridle, no saddle, and no barding on the horse.

"Have you ever used a sword before," the aide asked hurriedly.

"No," I hissed.

He took the sword from the scabbard and showed me how to handle it, stabbing instead of swinging since I had no experience with parrying thrusts. He then quickly showed me which areas were the most vulnerable – the underarm and groin.

"Remember, Lady, your uncle is the Prince of Darkness, your father is an archangel," he said. "Fighting is in your blood."

My hands shook as I accepted the sword and halberd. His words bolstered my confidence. He was right. I wasn't just a half-angel; I was a half-archangel. I remembered the thrill of seeing my father shooting towards the Earth in full battle mode only moments ago. Perhaps today would be the day I would make him proud.

"Beetle," I said, swallowing my fear. "I want you to join Geryon at Hell's Gate. It will be safer there for you."

"But I want to fight too," Beetle cried.

"I know, but you're still wounded and the gate must be held. There is nowhere safe tonight, but better there than here."

Beetle nodded and raced off to join the aide in exiting the far end of the stable. All that was left now was for me and Charlemagne and poor Binky to get going. I couldn't leave Binky alone.

Another cannon ball hit the ground outside the stable, this time causing the whole building to wobble. A beam only thirty feet from me dislodged from the roof and collapsed.

Charlemagne snorted and chomped at the bit.

"I know, we're going," I yelled over the sound of more cannon balls hitting the outer walls and stable yard.

"Come on, Binky, you're with us," I shouted as the drums of war sounded, the dukes and their one hundred legions readying to meet King Zagan and the traitorous dukes and their legions on the plains of Hell.

My fingers shook as I unlatched the stall door. Binky swung his head toward me and I patted his neck, leaning in to him and whispering a prayer for his and Charlemagne's safety. It was no use wishing for my own. As the duke had reminded me, I was a target, a target that had to protect itself.

I grabbed a foot stool and mounted Charlemagne, leaving the helmet the aide had brought me on a bale of hay. The slit was so narrow in the front I'd never be able to see out of it. I wrapped my legs around the warhorse and jogged out of the barn. It was a good thing I was tall as the warhorse stood over nineteen hands and was broad and fierce.

The once beautiful stable yard looked like a lunar landscape it was so full of large craters. The stable walls were filled with holes. Cracks marred the once splendid stonework. Acrid smoke filled the air. Rivers of lava ran down the mountains in the distance towards the plains where the battle for dominion over Hell had begun. The River Styx ran red. Fire raged in the southern end of Hell Town, some of the buildings already fallen as Zagan's army torched whatever they could. I hoped the seamstress would be okay.

I held the reins tightly in my fists as Charlemagne broke into a rocking horse canter, automatically heading for the plains where the legions had lined up like the pictures I'd seen in the history books of Gettysburg soldiers during the Civil War. Thousands would die this day.

Bile rose into my throat, but the words the young demon said to me echoed in my mind: your uncle is the Prince of Darkness, your father is an archangel - fighting is in your blood.

A hearty laugh burst from me as I realized that Charlemagne was adorned in Lucifer's colors from the dark ages, the purple hemp cloth beneath the silver armor the same color as my hair. Royal purple strands of silk hung from his bridle and billowed outwards from his tail. Lucifer's crest was a golden angel and a fire breathing dragon stitched into the purple saddle pad.

I grinned and let out the reins. The light grey destrier stretched into a gallop, ears forward, tail in the air, the bone horse beside us matching our pace stride for stride, stirrup leathers flapping. For an instant, I felt as if Lucas was with me. I drew my sword and let loose with a rebel yell.

"For Lucifer," I hollered.

The Challenge

The legions parted before me as I galloped to the front line where the dukes and generals were about to charge.

Death suddenly appeared on top of Binky, merging with the horse as if he had been riding beside me the whole time. Death's hemp cloak billowed out behind him. He held a sharpened scythe in his right hand. The edge glittered in the unearthly light cast by the volcanoes and wild fires rolling down the hills.

The legions of demons at our backs let out a monstrous wail, consumed by bloodlust. The ground shook as if rocked by a powerful earthquake, the sound so loud it almost burst my eardrums.

The dukes paused, waiting for Death and I to reach them.

"Well done, Mary Jane," Death congratulated me.

"I know who killed me," I said breathlessly as we waited for Duke Zepar to give the command.

"King Zagan," Death nodded.

"Yes," I said. "And Diana is part of it. She's joined Zagan's forces."

"Lucifer isn't going to like that," Death snorted.

"Speaking of my uncle," I said, admiring the fierce deity at my side. I had never seen Death looking so gallant. "Where is he?"

"You'll see," Death smirked. "Tonight, the prince rides a black stallion with fire in his heart."

"And his throat," I chuckled.

Death cast a sideways glance at me as Duke Zepar howled like a werewolf and put his spurs to Bucephalus.

"Charge," I boomed, slipping in beside the duke.

Charlemagne leapt forward with such force my pelvis slammed into the pommel.

"Death to the traitors," was the cry that rent the air.

"For the prince," I shouted again, the cry being taken up by the bloodthirsty hoards.

I unsheathed my sword and leaned forward into the charge, biting down on my tongue hard enough to draw blood, the pain keeping my fear at bay. Suddenly, the angel in me unfurled like a python awakening from a deep slumber. The savagery, the urge to kill, to maim, to send those who dared to rebel against my uncle, to oblivion took my breath away. I knew if I was to survive this day, I had to release the archangel in me, so I did.

Power coursed through my body. My wings elongated, expanding to near epic proportions, my feathers turning hard like tungsten steel, becoming weapons themselves. The sword in my hand felt like an extension of my arm.

Behind and beside me, demons screeched. The legions of soldiers in the rear vanguard raced across the plains behind the cavalry. Marquesse Andras and her thirty legions of Amazonian demons, all of whom were female and had feathered angel's wings and eagle heads soared overhead.

At the other side of the plains, King Zagan and the traitorous dukes charged in kind. Our air squadrons met Zagan's. Blood rained down from the skies as the marquesse's forces and the king's winged brigade battled for dominance.

Charlemagne doubled his speed as some of my energy trickled into the warhorse. Death and Binky fell behind.

Duke Zepar and Alocer parted as Charlemagne shot between them, their Hell horses no match for the renewed strength and speed of Lucifer's giant destrier. Duke Zepar nodded acquiescence as I met the onslaught of the first of Zagan's rebel forces head on.

The huntress was at the forefront of the demon line unleashing her arrows at the dukes behind me. They deflected the arrows easily with their mighty shields. Her powers weren't anywhere near as strong as she thought, not here on the duke's battle ground. She was out of her league and didn't even know it.

Energy coursed through my body as I cut through the mounted demons with my sword, the warhorse slashing and tearing into their horses as my enemies fell, my focus on getting to Diana. It was her arrow that slew me. It was her blood my archangel self screamed for. Charlemagne sensed it and redoubled his efforts.

The goddess turned from the soldier she fought to see me descending upon her. Diana slammed on the brakes, the bombshell of seeing my ten foot armored wingspan and gore-splattered sword and breastplate evident in the sudden fear flashing across her face.

Diana unleashed an arrow. I wrapped a wing in front of me to deflect it, but I needn't have.

My father, the archangel Gabriel, snatched the arrow out of the air and tossed it aside, a twisted grin on his face. I wanted to smash that grin right off of it. Fury burst out of me as I screamed: "She's mine!"

He shook his head and swerved to the right.

Brimstone shouldered Charlemagne out of the way as Lucifer burst through the lines. He winked at me as he passed. My anger dimmed as the shape-shifting Hell horse morphed into a dragon.

"I didn't do it, Lucifer," Diana wailed in fear. "Zagan did. He killed your niece!"

Ah, the truth was finally out. King Zagan used me to start this war. Sucks to be him, I chuckled ruthlessly.

Lucifer swung his sword in a wide arc as he descended upon the hapless deity. His wrath at being used and betrayed was titanic. An inferno transfigured both he and Brimstone into a blazing conflagration of cataclysmic proportions. It was impossible to see where dragon and archangel began and ended.

Demons on both sides leapt out of the way. Half of Zagan's army dropped their weapons and ran.

Diana threw down her arrows and slumped to the ground in defeat awaiting her demise. Her lips moved in prayer.

Lucifer's sword flashed, fire pirouetting up and down the blade. The sword finished its arc, but Diana was no longer there.

"Damn you, Zeus," Lucifer shrieked, pulling the dragon to a halt.

A lightning bolt rent the sky illuminating the mountains of fallen dead that littered the plains of Hell. Dazzling streaks of lightning blinded the living. Thunder peeled. Hell's six fallen archangels and fifteen heavenly archangel's fist bumped and saluted one another as the fighting came to an abrupt end.

King Zagan tried to run, one of his wings hanging crookedly by his side, but there was nowhere to go as the archangels herded him back towards the blazing Lucifer sitting astride his flaming dragon.

Out of the corner of my eye, I saw the strangest thing, and did a double-take thinking my eyes were playing a trick on me.

Three of the former *Ghost Rider Gang* approached me, Elijah and Ronin on horseback, and Caleb on foot. They were all armored and carrying swords. Elijah still wielded the angel's sword and wore Heaven's golden chainmail shirt to his advantage. Behind them scampered the outlaw want-to-be, Chappie.

"I see you joined Zagan's army," I seethed, Charlemagne prancing beneath me, steam billowing out of his nostrils.

"We had no choice," Caleb cried.

"There's always a choice, Caleb," I snarled.

"Time to die, Barney," Ronin jeered, trying to disarm me with his taunts.

It was no use; his barbed words meant nothing to me anymore. In releasing my archangel self, I found the courage to accept who and what I was. I may not be as pretty as all the rest of the archangels, but I was just as strong.

Death reined up beside me. His cloak was soaked in blood; his eyes coal black orbs, his expression bleak. I waved him aside and he backed away.

Caleb threw down his sword and stared hopelessly at his blood covered hands.

Chappie ran towards King Zagan, the coward.

I raised my sword and charged first Ronin and then Elijah. Ronin fell without fanfare and with an ease that shocked even me.

Elijah parried my thrusts, the heavenly forged sword sparking as it clashed with my hellfire sword. We battled, our horses circling, exchanging blows, until I saw an opening and lunged, sinking the short sword into his under arm and severing the artery. His eyes rounded in surprise when he fell from his horse. Lucas' brother or not, he was the demise of all of them.

One of the reapers scooped his soul from his body with a dreadful ripping sound and galloped away with it. I knew where Elijah was going, to the Hell Pits, but I did not pity him. We are all responsible for our choices, archangel, human and demon.

"I'm so sorry, Mary Jane," Caleb sniveled, laying a hand on my leg. "I don't know how Lucas and I could have gone along with Elijah and Ronin. They were so good at bullying and manipulating us both. I shall never forgive myself for not walking away."

My archangel wrath abated as if it were a weary traveler ready to slumber. I rested my sword across the pommel of my saddle. My arms ached and my body slumped with exhaustion, my wings retracting back into the tiny purple feathered ones I was used to. I was happy to see them.

"I know," I stammered, dismounting Charlemagne and gathering my love's best friend in my arms.

"You are as much a victim as I am," I comforted him. "I'll talk to my uncle when all this is done and see what I can do."

I surveyed the carnage around me and the dukes who even now were gathering up the demon rebels and escorting them off the battlefield in raggedy groups. The Marquesse and the archangels forced what was left of the winged demon brigades to surrender. Brimstone had returned to his preferred form, an elegant black stallion of noble heritage, but his rider remained as fearsome as always.

Too late, I noticed the deceitful king and his sidekick moving closer rather than farther away from Lucifer. Chappie retrieved the huntress' bow and arrow off the ground and tossed them to the king. Zagan snatched them out of the air, fletched and drew one of the golden arrows, drawing the bowstring back to his shoulder. With a predatory grin, he aimed the arrow not at Lucifer, but at me.

"Nooo," Caleb screamed, pushing me out of the way as the arrow flew towards its mark.

Diana's arrow penetrated Caleb's chest, much the same as the original arrow had mine. I caught him in my arms as his legs buckled and he crumbled to the ground.

Lucifer galloped the short distance to the king, raised his sword, and relieved King Zagan of both his head and his title. The king was no more. Long live the Prince of Darkness.

Similarly, Death spurred his skeletal steed forward, and wrapped his scythe around Chappie's throat. The Aussie's eyes went wide as his soul was destroyed.

"Are you sure you aren't Lucas' real brother," I blubbered, weeping for the brave cowboy I held close to my heart.

"I like to think so," he murmured, his eyes closing.

I heard the rumble of hoof beats. The Grim Reaper and Death crouched beside me. Lucifer and Brimstone's shadow towered over us.

"Let us do our jobs, sweetheart," Death said gently.

I nodded and stood up, leaving Caleb in my friends' capable hands.

"Would you like to accompany him," a deep voice intoned.

Startled, I looked up to see my father hovering above Lucifer. It was good to see Brimstone back to normal. I had to admit the dragon was handy, but daunting.

"I will gladly escort you to the gates if you want to accompany this soul to Heaven, daughter," Gabriel said, offering me his hand.

I inhaled deeply, shaken to the core at the way my father said, 'daughter'. It was heartfelt, warm, and a welcome relief to the cold shoulder he had always given me.

I turned to my uncle.

"Go ahead, Mary Jane, you've earned it," Lucifer nodded.

"Thank you, uncle," I smiled sadly up at him.

He nodded and backed Brimstone away from Caleb's wide-eyed soul and the group of archangels, deities and demons surrounding it.

"Up you go, Caleb," the Grim Reaper said, nodding towards Mr. Jeepers.

Caleb shook his head in disbelief as he looked down at his body, still confused by the turn of events.

The reaper sighed and mounted his horse. He held out a hand to help Caleb along.

Death nudged the soul forwards.

Caleb mounted Jeepers without comment.

I grabbed hold of my father's and we flew upwards alongside the Grim Reaper and Caleb aboard Mr. Jeepers. Caleb's grin was infectious as he held onto the Grim Reaper's waist, Mr. Jeepers taking it upon himself to take the long way around to the gates of Heaven.

"I'm proud of you," my father whispered as thirteen heavenly angels joined the escort, flying in a V formation behind us. It wasn't every day that a lost soul found redemption, let alone got an archangel escort, but I knew Caleb had the right stuff. He just had to find it, the same way that Lucas had. They had both unselfishly offered themselves up for another.

It was both sad and joyous how long I had waited to hear those words from my father. Perhaps it was too little too late, but the words rang hollow in my ears. It didn't matter anymore what my father thought of me, but what I thought of myself. I was proud of me too.

I wished Lucas were here to see it.

A sense of longing and loneliness overwhelmed me, so much so I feared I would topple out of the sky. I could ask my father to find Lucas and bring him to the Pearly Gates so we could see each other one more time.

I glanced sideways at my father. Gabriel was God's messenger. Would he be mine? The devil on my shoulder doubted it.

The Pearly Gates

The archangels who had joined the fight to save Hell waved goodbye and nodded to me in deference as they disappeared ahead of our little group before we reached the Pearly Gates.

Green forests and lush meadows dotted the landscape we flew over. I could see the Pearly Gates in the distance hovering in a cloud wrapped platform that rose above the beautiful scenery.

The closer we got, the broader the smile on my father's face became. It was odd feeling the warm grip of my father's hand still in mine. I should have been happier, but the loving grasp of a parent's hand in mine belonged to only one parent in my life, and that was my mother.

I tugged my hand out of his.

"I'll leave you to it," my father blushed as the gates swung open.

Had I just embarrassed God's favorite archangel?

I felt a bit guilty about that, but only a bit.

There was a sad wretch huddled against the wall outside of the Pearly Gates. He sat with his head down, hands across his knees, his hair limp and greasy. He looked oddly familiar.

I took in a deep breath and held it.

Could it be?

"I hear you've found your inner archangel," Saint Peter said to me.

I ignored him as I landed smoothly on the platform in front of the sitting figure. The wretch didn't look up.

Mr. Jeepers landed gently. Caleb slipped off the horse's back and offered his hand to the Grim Reaper. They shook hands as if they were long lost friends.

The sad form leaning against the wall seemed immune to the

heavenly choir beyond the golden gates singing a welcome to Caleb. Caleb was not. He bolted through the gates and ran into the arms of his family waiting on the other side.

"Lucas," I stammered.

The lost wretch raised his head at the mention of his name. Weary bloodshot eyes met mine. Realization dawned on Lucas' face and he jumped to his feet.

"Mary Jane," he sputtered, throwing his arms around me. "I couldn't go in. I can't spend eternity without you."

"He refused to enter Heaven even after I told him what you were," Peter sneered. "You will never set foot beyond these gates, not on my watch. This silly fool has been sitting here mooning for you ever since. I haven't the foggiest idea why."

I smothered the urge to blow a raspberry at Saint Peter or flip him the bird, but two wars in one afterlife was enough for me right now.

"I don't want to spend eternity without you either," I laughed, leaning my head against Lucas' shoulder. "I'm sorry I never told you I was a half-angel, make that half-archangel."

"I don't care, I love you," Lucas murmured, holding me close.

"I love you too, but I only have half a soul so I can't ever enter Heaven. I can't ask you to return to Hell with me," I sobbed. "It wouldn't be fair."

"I'm not going anywhere without you," he said stubbornly, planting a kiss on my forehead. "I fell in love with you the day I saw you fly over top of Leyland's head to land ass-over-teakettle in a water jump, get up, limp soaking wet over to a camera and take a bow like you had planned the whole thing."

I snorted back the tears. I wished I'd met him before we both died.

"You have to walk through those gates," I groaned. "You don't belong in Hell."

"I belong with you," he said, adamant.

I whistled lightly as I left out a long deep breath.

What were we going to do? We couldn't sit outside the Pearly Gates forever.

"You need to leave, Nephilim" Peter exclaimed. "Now or I'll call Michael!"

"Don't bother, I'm already here," the archangel Michael laughed landing with a thump on the platform beside me.

Another archangel landed behind him.

My eyes widened in surprise.

"See you later, bro," Michael said, slapping Lucifer good-naturedly on the back. "Stay out of trouble, will you?"

"I doubt it," Lucifer grinned.

"Chill, Peter," Michael chortled, giving me a wink before strutting through the gates.

Peter slammed the gates shut behind the archangel. The saint looked like he had just sucked on a lemon.

"So, we have a stalemate," my uncle said. "Lucas won't go to Heaven without you and you can't get into Heaven even with my illustrious influence."

Saint Peter sputtered in indignation.

"Stand up straight, both of you," Lucifer ordered us, ignoring the irate saint.

I turned to Lucas. He looked just as bewildered as me.

"I don't have much time so, Lucas Wells, do you take Mary Jane Bligh to be your wife and to love and to cherish her so long as she resides in Hell," he asked Lucas.

Saint Peter was about to object, but Lucifer raised a hand in warning, Death suddenly appearing by the saint's side to enforce it.

"I do," Lucas grinned stupidly.

"Mary Jane Bligh, do you take Lucas Wells to be your husband and to love and to cherish... yadayadayada... so long as he resides in Hell," my uncle said, looking askance at me.

"I do," I squealed, my wings fluttering of their own accord.

"Then by the power invested in me as the Prince of Darkness, I now pronounce you man and wife," Lucifer finished. "And now, I have to get back to Hell, so many to punish and so much time to do it. And don't forget you have a stable to manage, my dear."

"No, I don't, it's fallen down," I laughed.

"Not for long," my uncle chuckled.

"Congratulations you two," Death remarked dryly. "And if you ever break her heart, I will end your existence, Lucas Wells."

I rolled my eyes in Death's direction but he was already gone, as was my uncle.

Lucas kissed me.

I couldn't wait to go home. My heart was full; my life in eternity was looking better and better. My mother was going to be so happy.

Oh, oh!

I was in deep doo-doo.

There was an angry cough behind us.

"Oh, right," I said, shrugging helplessly. "We can't stay here."

"What do we do now," Lucas grinned. "Where in Hell can we go for a honeymoon? Gosh, I never thought I'd ever say that."

"I have a couple of ideas," I giggled gleefully, spreading my wings.

The sun caught them at just the right angle so as to reflect a rainbow of colorful shades of pink, blue and purple.

I wrapped my hand around my husband's and we dove off the platform, falling, falling, falling… into our future together.

If you enjoyed this novella, please consider leaving an honest review on Amazon, Bookbub or Goodreads, or your own media pages. It means a lot to all authors if you spread the word about books you enjoyed.

If you want to hear about upcoming releases including the next novel in this series, then visit Laura's blog at www.Running L Productions.com or on Facebook, Amazon, Bookbub or Goodreads.

List of Hell's Inhabitants

Demon list:

- Zagan : Demon King, deceitful and conniving. He commands 33 legions.

- Zepar : Grand Duke, a straight as an arrow type of soldier who commands 26 legions. His horse is Bucephalus – won him from Alexander in a poker game: black with a large white star on his forehead.

- Andras : Marquesse, commands 30 legions; bird head with angel-like wings

- Alocer : Knight of Hell, black armor. He commands 36 legions and has a lion's head.

- Berith : Knight of Hell, red armor and rides a red horse named Wild Fire. He governs 26 legions.

- Geryon : Giant centaur, guardian of hell

4 Horsemen of the Apocalypse: Conquest, War, Famine and Death.

Death: Binky is the bone horse owned by Death. Death is an immortal being that lives and breathes like a human.

Grim Reaper: He's very sweet and caring when it comes to his horse Mr. Jeepers.

Other Books by Laura Hesse

The Holiday Series (family adventure):
*One Frosty Christmas, The Great Pumpkin Ride, A Filly
Called Easter, Independence and Valentino*

Paranormal Thriller:
The Thin Line of Reason

The Gumboot & Gumshoe Series (Amusing Cozy Mystery):
Book One: *Gumboots, Gumshoes & Murder*
Book Two: *The Dastardly Mr. Deeds*
Book Three: *Murder Most Fowl*
Book Four: *Gertrude & The Sorcerer's Gold*
Book Five: *Chasing Santa*

The Silver Spurs Series (Naughty Western Satire):
*The Silver Spurs Home for Aging Cowgirls
Bandits, Broads & Dirty Dawgs
Who Killed Cade*

Paranormal Romance
Lucifer and Mary Jane: All The Devil's Horses

Find out more about upcoming releases on Laura's website
@ www.RunningLProductions.com and hit the "Follow
Me" button or follow Laura on Goodreads or Bookbub.

About the Author

Laura lives on Vancouver Island with a rescue dog and an old cat. She grew up a back stage brat in Music Hall Theatre and credits her mother with her love of the Arts. She loves to sing at local jams when she can.

Laura spent many happy years riding the trails and writes about the special horses in her life within the pages of her novels. While Sally and all the rest have passed over the rainbow, they will forever live on in her stories.

Peace and wellness to all.